Rescuing the Reluctant Groom

DISCARD

by

Barbara Lohr

Purple Egret Press

Purple Egret Press
Savannah, Georgia 31411

This book is a work of fiction. The characters, events and places in the book are products of the author's imagination and are either fictitious or used fictitiously. Any similarity of real persons, living or dead, is purely coincidental and not intended by the author.

Cover Art: The Killion Group
Editing: The Editing Hall

Print ISBN: 978-0-9908642-6-4
Digital ISBN: 978-0-9908642-5-7

for

Ted

Chapter 1

A cold sun batted its head against the frosted bedroom windows. Winter in Chicago and the temperature hovered around ten degrees outside. Somewhere in Oak Park, church bells tolled. The weather might be freezing but contentment warmed Selena's heart. Rolling over in bed, she traced a finger down Seth's back. The man barely moved. Cocooned under the quilt, she snuggled closer to his heat. *Madre de Dios*, this felt good.

If she poked her nose above the covers and exhaled, her breath might form a cloud. Outside, car tires whined, spinning on the ice. Selena sure wasn't anxious to get out there. *Que bueno* that today was McKenna's turn to be on call for their midwifery practice.

Like always, Seth had kicked off the comforter. The man was a walking space heater. He lay curled on his tummy like a baby, except babies didn't have muscles like his. Seth Kirkpatrick was a babe, not a *niño*. The man was strong enough to load a stretcher into an ambulance himself, gentle enough to calm an accident victim. Her man was all heart.

Dark stubble accented his square chin and framed his sculpted lips. The auburn Kirkpatrick hair was shaved shorter on the side. Oh yeah, he was a bad boy and Selena should feel darn lucky. Instead, frustration chipped at her peace, like an ice scraper against the frosted window.

"*Te amo*, you maddening man," she whispered. Bells still rang in the early morning air, happy as wedding bells. Her hands and heart felt restless. She danced her fingertips over Seth's strong nose, skimmed the full lips.

Wedding bells and babies?

What was with her today?

With a sleepy mumble, Seth hugged her tight. Face pressed against the pillow, he was dreaming. She chuckled when he wrinkled his forehead, like he was trying to tell one of his stories. Most times, he couldn't remember the punch line. Seth got so mad when that happened. Pushing up on an elbow, she watched him.

Que guapo. Her man was so gorgeous.

Was Seth hers? Sometimes she wondered. Sure, he could talk about medical conditions with patients. *No problema.* But when it came to feelings and their relationship? Not so good.

The words she'd been waiting for? Selena heard them only in her dreams.

Eyes still closed, he ran a warm hand from her shoulder to one hip.

"Oh, *mi amor.*" She squirmed with pleasure.

"Sissy…" he breathed.

"*Sissy?*" Selena sprang up so fast, the quilt slid to the floor. Frigid air seared her skin like dry ice. Had her heart stopped beating? She swatted at him. "*Qué dices?* What did you just say about Sissy?"

Rubbing his eyes, Seth mumbled, "Sissy who? Sissy Hanson?"

Sí, I'm having a heart attack.

A frown appeared above his dark eyes. The bells had stopped. All joy had been sapped from the room. "What are you talking about, babe? Huh? Come here, Selena."

That husky morning voice usually worked Selena like a loofah sponge. Not this morning. *Sissy?* The name still rang in her ears. Blonde hair, blue eyes and a body that even made that navy EMS uniform look sexy. Standing beside the bed, Selena felt stiff as a cemetery stone. She crossed her arms across her heaving chest.

Then she got mad.

"You! *Idiota! Mi madre me dijo que...*" Words that would make her mother blush flowed like lava. Still wasn't enough. Grabbing a pillow, Selena started swinging.

"Hey, stop! What are you doing?" Seth struggled to sit up.

She tossed the pillow but not the anger. Selena pressed her trembling lips together. No way would she let Seth see her cry. Reaching down, she grabbed her clothes from the cold hardwood floor. Woke her up fast, that's for sure, and made her madder than ever.

"What are you doing?" Sitting up, Seth scratched his head.

"I'm leaving. You never tell me you love me. *Nunca.* Never. I'm a fool. And now this Sissy thing? Really?"

"Sissy Hanson?"

"Ah, hah!" Leaning over, Selena stabbed his chest with one finger, wishing her nails were longer. "So you admit it."

"Admit what?" He ran a hand across the muscular chest now imprinted with her fingernail. How could that one move turn her on? Selena's anger kicked up a notch.

"So you like her blonde hair, eh? That cute dimple? How long has this been going on? All those nights together working the late shift?" How could a man look so adorable when his hair was a mess and he had sleepers in his eyes?

He shoved up onto an elbow. "What are you taking about, woman?"

"First word out of your mouth this morning. Sissy. Oh, Sissy." Lips pursed together, she gave a great imitation, even though Seth hadn't said the name *quite* like that.

Seth's lips moved but no words came to comfort her.

Shoving her head into her sweatshirt, Selena swept two rubber bands from the night table and yanked her hair into pigtails. "*Perfecto*. Deny it, go ahead. Tell me you're not fooling around with her."

Seth looked at her like she'd grown two heads. "Selena, baby, I'm asking you… what *is* going on?"

Normally Selena would melt when Seth blinked those long eyelashes that no man should have. Not today. She held up two fingers. "*Dos años*. Two years together and you still can't use the L word. But you can moan about Sissy. Oh, sure. *See-see*. Well, she can have you!"

Ah, hah! That got him up. Trying to find his jeans, he hopped around on the cold floor. Seth's muscular legs flexing in the dim light almost made her weaken. But not this time. Instead, she kicked his jeans farther under the bed.

"Selena, honey, that's not true. Stop being so crazy."

"*Loca?* Me?" Grabbing the cowhide purse he'd given her for

Christmas, she raced for the stairs. "We are over. *Finito.*"

She should have done this a long time ago. Should've left him the first time she told him she loved him and he just looked at her. Right, he'd stared at her like she'd ordered a meal not on his menu. Clutching the bannister so she wouldn't fall, she gulped back her tears. No way would she let him see her cry.

Maybe Seth Kirkpatrick never would settle down. Maybe he'd always be a ladies' man, the *muchacho guapo* every woman wanted.

Shoving her feet into her suede boots, Selena tore her silver quilted jacket from the front hall closet. Stumbling to the head of the stairs, Seth was having a hard time getting into his jeans. "For cripes' sake, Selena. Wait."

Glancing into the kitchen, she saw the red Fiesta dishes she'd set out last night. The ones she'd bought him for Christmas, so bright and cheerful for the holidays. McKenna, Seth's sister and Selena's good friend, had teased her. "You got dishes for my brother? That's so cute, Selena. Is this part of his hope chest?"

Cute. So perfect for a couple on Sunday morning—plates for eggs and toast, the red mugs ready next to the coffee machine.

Grabbing one of the plates, she turned.

Now halfway down the steps, Seth came to a halt. "Selena?"

A flick of her wrist sent the dish soaring like a frisbee. He ducked. *Qué lástima.* Barely missing one of his Frank Lloyd Wright sketches, it shattered against the wall. Seth's hands shot out, palms up. "Selena, honey. Please."

A mug felt so good in her hand. Heavy enough to hurt. "Please? *Please, Selena,*" she mimicked him. *"I love to hear you beg."*

This time she took aim. The mug hit his arm and ricocheted to the bannister before crashing to the floor. But hurting Seth hurt her. She paused, but not for long. This morning, her own pain felt worse.

Seth picked his way over the broken pieces. "Ouch. Crap. Are you crazy?"

"*Loca, sí!*" *Crazy enough to fall in love with you.* Another mug. But he dodged again. For a big man, Seth could be quick on his feet. *Crash.* She smiled and considered the sugar bowl. That piece had been hard to find. And he was close to the bottom of the staircase.

Racing from the kitchen, she yanked open the front door. Icy air blasted her face. Jacket not zipped, she didn't even feel the cold. After she slammed the door behind her with a bang, she heard Seth swearing a blue streak. Taking a deep breath, she smiled.

A frozen world greeted her. Snow fell softly, catching in her hair and squeaking beneath her boots. She tried to be careful hurrying to her sports vehicle. At least it started. Leaving the engine running, she popped the back open, grabbed a brush and cleared the windows. Cold snow blew back into her face. They didn't call Chicago the Windy City for nothing.

Tears blinded her by the time she climbed back into her car. Seth hadn't come after her. Clutching her chest, she breathed in and tried to calm her breaking heart. Then she floored it.

Seth's front door opened just as she squealed away from the curb.

"Selena! Wait!" Is that what she heard?

No more waiting. The SUV fishtailed and then shot down the

street.

Sunday morning and the streets were quiet under the fresh mantel of snow. Newspapers were embedded in white lawns and driveways. Eyes blurred with tears, she eased up on the gas. Last thing she needed was a ticket or an accident. When she reached Harlem Avenue, she turned north toward the Eisenhower Expressway. It was too early for bumper-to bumper traffic. The leaden gray sky was turning pearl pink. Sniffling back her tears, she switched on the radio. Thank goodness the song that blasted was Adele. Something about burning so bad after she broke up with her man. *Perfecto.*

Selena ratcheted up the music until her ears rang.

She'd broken those expensive dishes. Really? She busted out laughing.

Right now Seth was sipping coffee at his breakfast bar, watching sports highlights on TV. He probably thought she'd get over it, like always. He'd grab the dustpan and sweep up the broken dishes, along with pieces of her heart.

Later he'd stop over, lean in her doorway like the hottie that he was and give her an I'm-so-sorry smile. Embarrassing, but that had worked in the past. Her anger always melted like snow in March.

But this was January.

What made this different, besides the Sissy thing?

They were at the two-year mark. Within two years, a woman knows if he's a keeper. Well, Selena knew. She wanted Seth Kirkpatrick for the rest of her life. But maybe he didn't feel that way. How that hurt. Popping her console open, she grabbed a tissue.

Did she think he actually had a thing with Sissy, the cute EMT on his emergency medical services squad? Not really, and some of the pain eased with her sigh. Still, the fact that he'd used Sissy's name, even in a dream, made her head pound. Stoked up again, anger flowed through her, igniting every nerve ending along the way. She banged her hands against the steering wheel to ease the pain in her heart.

But she better watch it. Her palms throbbed. These hands delivered babies, her life's work.

Only one place for her this morning, so she headed for Montclair Hospital. No way could she go home to her apartment and sit there alone on this cold Sunday. At the office, she could update the charts Dorothy had left on her desk. Hardly any traffic clogged the Magnificent Mile when she hit Michigan Avenue. Trees strung with tiny white lights, the area always looked like Christmas.

This year the holidays had brought so many good things to the Kirkpatrick family. Her good friend McKenna had become engaged to Logan Castle, the head of OB at Montclair. Sure, she was happy for McKenna. Six months and Logan popped the question.

Selena wanted to be next. She envisioned a ring on her finger that said Seth loved her forever. But she might have gray hair before he said those words. Sure, sometimes he'd toss out a "Love ya" before they hung up. How she longed for a lot more than that, but she'd be happy with "I love you, Selena. Will you marry me?"

She couldn't wait forever.

The ache in her heart pooled in her empty stomach. Maybe she'd never eat again.

She drummed her fingers on the steering wheel, waiting for the light to change. Collars turned up against the winter wind, visitors strolled past sparkling windows. But Selena couldn't feel the joy. Her mood felt as heavy as the parking meters. Had she wasted two years with Seth Kirkpatrick? After all, she was twenty-seven. She sure didn't want to be like McKenna and reach thirty with no prospects in sight. Babies didn't always come easy. Look at Connor, the oldest in the Kirkpatrick clan, and his wife Amanda. Getting pregnant had taken over five years and left them broke.

This past winter they'd adopted a baby whose young, unmarried mother had been in McKenna's natural childbirth class. Meanwhile, the in vitro treatments at Logan's infertility clinic finally kicked in for Connor and Amanda. They were pregnant with twins and suddenly Kirkpatrick babies were everywhere.

But not for Selena.

When she reached the parking garage of the hospital, she took the ramp slowly to the top level, where snow mounded around the wheels of McKenna's red jeep. She must have had a delivery last night. Jumping out of her SUV, Selena listened to the waves rumbling below. Lake Michigan thundered against the ice floes that formed along the shore, heavy, dark and cold.

Cheeks prickling from the icy wind, Selena wiped her nose on her jacket sleeve just like her *mamacita* told her never to do. Today she felt like breaking every rule.

Wasn't she made of tougher stuff than this? All those hot

summers detassling corn and picking cherries as a migrant worker had taught her one thing. She could survive anything. With or without Seth Kirkpatrick, she would have a better life. Turning on her heel, she locked her car with one click and hurried toward the elevator shaft.

Her phone pinged and she checked it while she waited. Sure. Seth would now bombard her with texts. The silver doors opened and she crammed the phone back in her pocket.

Taking the elevator down to the third floor, she marched across the overpass and into the medical office building attached to the hospital. The empty hallways spooked her on weekends. Unlocking the door of For Women, she entered the deserted waiting room, now lit by one lamp they left on for the cleaning staff. Chairs lined the walls, along with low tables stacked with magazines full of Hollywood gossip.

Stretching along the far side, a huge bulletin board was papered with snapshots of babies—their Wall of Fame. She never got tired of looking at those pictures. During the week, this room was crowded with women. This morning, no patients waited to register at the high counter where their receptionist Dorothy usually sat.

The practice was growing. For Women had three midwives, two nurse practitioners and two medical assistants, all drawn by natural techniques like water birth. She headed back into the exam area. When she saw the light on in McKenna's office, her steps slowed.

Facing McKenna right now might be hard. But her office was empty and relief flooded through her. Head down, Selena continued on and unlocked her own door. Unzipping her jacket, she tossed it over a chair, dropped her purse on the floor and collapsed into the desk chair.

How had Seth become such a heartbreak?

Turning on her computer, Selena scanned the admissions. Yep, Melanie Turner had her baby last night. Their patients rotated through the practice, eventually seeing all three midwives. But McKenna had been Melanie's main contact. Melanie and Richard were a cute couple who had waited a long time for this baby, kind of like Connor and Amanda.

But Selena was getting ahead of herself. Why worry about babies when she couldn't even land the man? She was reading the Sunday memo from Warren, their CEO, when the outer door opened. Five seconds later, McKenna stood in her doorway. Selena's throat closed just looking at the woman who would never be her sister-in-law. Man, she couldn't even get the words out. No way would she cry on McKenna's shoulder, but she sure needed her advice.

McKenna's smile slid from her face. "Hey, girlfriend. What's going on?"

A sniffle was all Selena could manage.

McKenna's arms opened. Pushing back her chair, Selena walked into her friend's warm comfort. She was seriously in need of some sisterly love. "Hate to tell you, McKenna. But it's Seth."

"No way. What has he done?"

"Sissy Hanson. That's what or who he's done."

McKenna's loud gasp could probably be heard in the main building. "No way. Seth would never do that to you. Where did

11

you hear this?"

Taking her seat, Selena poured out the sad story. "You're probably right, McKenna. This may have been just a dream— although I think he should dream about me. But things aren't looking good."

"My younger brother can be a knucklehead." Stunned didn't quite cover McKenna's expression as she plopped into the wingchair and listened to Selena's story about shattering the new dinnerware in an all-out assault on Seth.

"You mean the ones you just gave him for Christmas?"

Selena wiggled her eyebrows. "Bad right?"

They both laughed until tears came.

Then the chuckles died in Selena's throat. "Seth's not coming around with a ring like Logan. He's not even offering me the L word."

McKenna's jaw dropped. "Are you kidding me? Selena, that's crazy. You are gorgeous, funny and smart. I can think of maybe ten other guys who'd stand in line for a date with you. Go for it."

And this was from Seth's own sister? "What are you saying?"

"Seth doesn't even tell you he loves you? He's going to be thirty, for Pete's sake. The boy better take a good look at his life and what he wants."

A rock plummeted to the bottom of Selena's stomach. "Guess it's not me."

Grabbing Selena's hand, McKenna squeezed hard. "Trust me, he *does* want you. You just have to remind him of that."

"How?"

McKenna's lips tilted into a devious smile. "Plotting Seth's wake up call will give me something else to think about..."

"Right. Besides your wedding? *Caramba*, McKenna. That should be your main concern right now, not my problems."

McKenna's engagement to the hottest doc on staff made Selena so happy. She'd been with them on their mission trip to Guatemala the summer before, the week that really sealed their romance. Why couldn't Seth have Logan's certainty?

"Seth never tells you he loves you?" McKenna's forehead wrinkled.

"It's more a 'Love ya, babe' thing."

The sound from McKenna's lips gave Selena the giggles. She did the best strawberry ever.

"And the worst part is, this isn't the first time I've broken up with Seth. He might not take me seriously." Selena couldn't resist looking at her pinging phone, where texts kept popping up.

Still mad at me? Don't be. Please.

And also:

Hated to get out of bed this morning without your wakeup call.

Uh huh. She knew exactly what Seth meant and her body reacted.

Finally:

Want to come over and watch the game this afternoon? We can talk.

Right. Talking during a basketball game. That would never happen.

Seth wasn't good at talking. Period.

"Show him you mean business." McKenna's face brightened.

She was such a great idea person. The specialized birthing unit now under construction had been her brainchild, although at first Logan had fought it. As head of OB at Montclair, he could be conservative.

"How can I show him anything? I told him I never wanted to see him again."

Of course she would see Seth again. Every time an EMS Limited ambulance pulled into the Montclair ER, there was a good chance Seth would be on it. She couldn't avoid him forever.

Getting to her feet, McKenna strolled to the window and began to etch hearts into the white frost. Despite the maintenance department's work, the windows in this building continued to frost over. "Stay in his face, Selena. Don't give up, okay?"

"I'm not a quitter."

"That's right. Resilience. That's what you teach those women in Guatemala." McKenna smiled at her window handiwork. "And you're a good friend. You even come to Sunday dinner at my parents' house."

"When Seth and I were together. I'm not coming today."

"Why not?" McKenna tried to look all innocent.

"Because I can't? Because I'd like to pick up a kitchen knife when I think of Seth and Sissy."

McKenna's chuckles echoed in the small office. "Make it uncomfortable for him."

Selena's phone pinged again and her chest tightened. "I don't know if I can do this. Not today."

"Maybe you're right. Give my family time to needle him. They know the drill with Seth. Growing up, he had to have everything the other boys had. If Connor got a new lunch bucket, Seth had to have one too."

"But Connor's the oldest."

"Seth never got over it. A middle child who had some, er, issues." McKenna stumbled a bit but before Selena could get a question in, her friend roared on. "He'd gripe to my mother and usually got what he wanted."

"Reenie does fuss about him." Selena loved the family's nickname for Maureen Kirkpatrick. "I like to hear how it was with your family growing up." For Selena, the rowdy family seemed almost magical.

McKenna shrugged. "We're like most families, I think."

"How can you say that? Growing up, I never went to one school. You were at St. Edmund's from first grade to fifth grade, right?"

McKenna shrugged. "Sure. We all were. Even my mom went to that school."

They were talking about different planets. Time to set the record straight. "We moved all the time, McKenna. Like any migrant family, we followed the crops from Texas to Michigan and then back down again. We were always changing schools. I never had a best friend."

The last comment brought a gasp. "Oh my God, Selena. I knew you worked on a farm but..."

"Not a farm. Many farms." Had she said too much? This felt so embarrassing but McKenna was her best friend, the one she never

Barbara Lohr

had growing up. "If we stopped at a store for bread and peanut butter after working all day, people would stare at our dirty clothes. When my mother spoke to us, our names confirmed what they suspected. We were 'illegals' in everyone's eyes. For a while I even considered changing my name. Selena, Rafael. Our names made us different."

"But I love your names. They make you special."

And that's why she adored McKenna. "That's not how the rest of the world sees it. Anyway, here in Chicago I felt like I finally belonged." For the first time in her life, she fit in and she wanted it to stay that way.

Remembering those early years took effort. The adrenaline drained from Selena's body and she felt so darn tired. What a good time she'd had with Seth the night before. They hadn't done anything special. Just watched an action movie on Seth's big-screen TV, the one the family camped in front of for every sporting event or race.

The Kirkpatricks always made her feel welcome. Bringing her crockpot over, Selena would make a huge pot of her mother's Mexican chili, bubbling with tons of hot peppers. In fact, that crockpot was still in Seth's cupboard.

Uncoupling wasn't going to be easy.

"Seth always loved my chili," she murmured, twining a curl around her finger.

McKenna's boisterous laugh lifted Selena's spirits. "He's gonna miss way more than that."

Snatching Seth's photo from her desk, Selena shoved it into a drawer. "Oh, I hope so."

~.~

Pushing open his parents' front door, Seth stamped the snow from his boots before stepping inside. The smell of his mother's pot roast reminded him that he hadn't eaten all day. Food? Last thing on his mind. Toeing off his boots, he left them on the mat along with the others. His mom had cooked one of his favorites and he wasn't hungry. Maybe he had the flu.

Who was he kidding? This thing with Selena had him worried. She hadn't answered her phone or texted him back all day. And that mess at home? It took him a while to clean up the broken dishes.

What a woman. He'd never seen her this angry. In a weird way, it turned him on.

"How's my handsome boy?" Hurrying from the kitchen, his mom wiped her hands on her apron before lifting her cheek for a kiss. She smelled like onions and *Charlie*, the perfume she asked for every Christmas.

"Hi, Mom." He tried to smile.

She peered closer. "What's wrong?"

Dammit. "N-nothing." He gave her a tight hug and backed off.

"Seth? What are you keeping from me?" She had him by the forearms, but no way did he want to mention this thing with Selena. With any luck, he'd have everything sorted out in a few days.

"You worry too much, Mom. Nothing."

Thank God Mark and Connor, two of his brothers, arrived just in time from the back family room. "How's the boy?" Connor cuffed him on the shoulder. The squalling upstairs was probably from Sean, Connor's newly adopted son.

"You're not looking so good." Mark narrowed his eyes. "Big night out?"

"Nope. Not really." Enough of this. Escaping, he marched into the living room where two of his sisters-in-law were having a heart-to-heart on the sofa. Girl talk. Bad timing.

With a wave, he escaped to the kitchen. Big mistake. McKenna was cleaning the carrots at the sink. Last person he wanted to see. Sugar-burned carrots were one of his favorites. Not today.

"How's it going, little brother?"

"F-fine." As if to prove it, he grabbed a carrot and munched down. His stomach did a weird twist but he kept chewing.

"You're really going to tell me everything's fine?"

So the word was out. Damn. He could hardly swallow.

His mother bustled into the kitchen behind them. "What's going on?"

McKenna's eyes skewered him. "You'll have to ask Seth."

With a growl, he barreled toward the family room, high-fived his dad and said hi to Logan.

"Hey, how's it going?" Logan looked up.

"Don't start." Grabbing a can of pop from a bucket of ice in the corner, he plopped onto the sofa.

Feet up on a hassock, his dad looked as amazed as his future brother-in-law. "Get up on the wrong side of the bed, son?"

A retired fireman, his father had never been good at heart-to-heart talks. Seth was not about to go into the Selena thing with him. And Logan? If he hadn't asked McKenna to marry him last Christmas, Seth wouldn't be in this situation. He wouldn't be here alone.

This was all Logan's fault. He grabbed some pretzels from the bowl on the coffee table and crunched down hard. The TV blared but his dad and Logan weren't even watching it. Instead, they were giving him weird looks.

"Could we just watch the g-game?" Pretzels in hand, Seth settled in, just as he did every Sunday. But everything felt different. "What's the score?"

His dad was still giving him the fish eye and Logan? Was that a grin?

Amanda appeared in the doorway behind the sofa. Sean, her adopted son, was cradled in her arms. Four months pregnant with twins and she already looked like she could deliver any day. Connor came up behind her, crooning at his new son. He'd never seen his brother like this. The whole place smelled of baby powder and poop, and Connor was all googly-eyed.

"Where's Selena?" Amanda glanced around.

Seth jumped up so damn fast he made the baby cry.

"Hey dude, baby in the house." Connor took the baby from Amanda and started patting him on the back.

"Sorry, Amanda. Connor." Feeling terrible, Seth wished he could comfort the baby. But he couldn't. Not today. He'd probably drop the kid.

From the look on Connor's face, Seth knew he'd be given the

third degree later. Connor took his role as oldest in the family seriously. Seth started to sweat. Why did his parents always pump the heat up so high?

Downstairs where the pool table was set up, the kids' voices rose above the crack of the balls. Usually Seth liked hanging out with his nephews and niece. Today the noise was getting on his nerves.

Wheeling around, he headed back into the kitchen. "You look like you've seen a ghost, son." His mother was tending the carrots sizzling in the pan. Smelled like biscuits in the oven, another one of his favorites. His stomach growled but nausea made it impossible to think of eating.

"Aw, Mom. I don't think it's a ghost that's bothering him. Is it, Seth?" Lifting the cover of the slow roaster, McKenna poked the meat with her fork. Her sly grin told him she knew. Cornered, he felt like he was in a speeding ambulance and the patient wasn't responding.

"Nothing is bothering me, okay?" Maybe he needed a beer, not pop. Tossing his empty can into the trash, he grabbed a beer from the refrigerator, twisted off the top and took a cool sip. It tasted like vinegar and his stomach lurched.

He should have stuck with the pretzels.

"What's the matter, Seth?" A smile played along his sister's lips. She was loving his discomfort. Had she told their mother anything? That would be out of bounds.

He did what any man would do. Kept quiet. He was edging toward the door when McKenna turned, "Hey, how's Sissy Hanson doing?"

His mother's head jerked. "Who is Sissy?"

"N-no one. Just someone I work with."

"Long blonde hair," McKenna murmured while his mother's mouth fell open. "She wears it in a braid down her back. Does she ever unbraid that thing, Seth?"

Spatula in hand, his mother fisted her hands on her hips. "Seth Michael Kirkpatrick, what have you been doing?" Looked like she just might use that spatula on him, the way she did years ago when she caught him raiding the cookie jar.

"Nothing." His arms flew out, sending the damn beer all over the kitchen.

With a smug smile, McKenna handed him a roll of paper towels. "That's about right, Mom. He's been doing absolutely nothing. Better clean up your mess, Seth."

Chapter 2

When Selena pushed open the heavy wooden door of the Purple Frog, she could feel the music clear through to her teeth. Fine, bring it on. Anything to knock Seth out of her head. If he would just stop calling and texting. She sent him straight to voicemail.

Maybe she'd listen later. Probably more than once.

She was tempted to print off the texts. Now, how pathetic was that?

Forgetting Seth? Not working out so well.

McKenna stood up and waved from a back booth. Easy to see her red hair, even in the low light. Peanut shells crunched underfoot as Selena plowed her way through the crowd. A few folks from the hospital greeted her.

"Where's Seth?" Livvy Wright from OB asked.

A shrug was Selena's answer. She had to get used to this and soldiered on toward the back.

When she reached the booth, Vanessa and Amy were already there.

"Hey girl, where you been?" McKenna scooted over and Selena sat down.

"Had a hard time finding a place to park. Vanessa. Amy." She gave McKenna's friends from high school a smile. Tonight they were going to talk about McKenna's May wedding. Felt like rubbing salt in the wound, but Selena stretched a stiff smile across her face.

A pitcher of beer and four frosty mugs arrived. McKenna poured and then raised her glass. "To my good friends. Celebrating all our problems with men because they always work out in the end." The pointed glance was meant for Selena but she buried her nose in her mug.

Work out? With a man who put the capital S on stubborn? Not likely.

"You got that right. Alex got so high-handed with me when he was trying to claim Bo. I want to pop him over the head." Vanessa's smile softened. "Then we got married and my baby girl Melody came along."

"How is your little girl doing?" Heat flooded Selena's face. She had to build a fortress around her heart when it came to babies.

"Melody's great. Slept through the night after the second week. But Bo? Definitely some sibling rivalry."

They all laughed but for Selena, it felt hollow. Their waiter swung by again and skimmed a basket of peanuts onto the table. The conversation turned to bridesmaid dresses. When the music kicked up, so did their voices. Donna Summers was breathing and panting. The sexy sounds took Selena back to making love with Seth. Memories knifed her and she took a deep breath.

McKenna broke into a raucous laugh. "Wait a minute. This song was playing the first time I met Logan outside of work. We came here. Talk about the conversation warming up."

More chuckles, then McKenna slid an apologetic glance in Selena's direction. Maybe it was her Latin heritage but Selena could never mask her feelings. Seth had liked that about her. "My hot chili pepper," he'd teased her.

Right now her smile felt splintered around the edges.

Vanessa tilted her head to one side. "Maybe the song could give me some pointers. "Once you have two kids, things change."

"Those night feedings will do it to you every time." Amy's eyes were ringed with fatigue.

"How old is Gianna now?" Selena asked.

"About ten months."

"I delivered her last spring, remember?" McKenna's smile turned misty, like she might be thinking of the babies she'd have with Logan. Selena's eyes stung and she blinked furiously. Although McKenna had delivered Amy's baby, Selena had been one of the first to see Gianna. So perfect and delicate.

Parenting might take a lot out of a woman but Selena was ready for it. For years, she'd watched her own mother have baby after baby. She still went to the fields, a *rebozo* tied around one shoulder with the infant tucked inside.

"Amy, does Melody still keep you up at night?" She struggled to look interested while Amy launched into the details of night feedings and misplaced pacifiers. Her mind conjured up little red-haired kids who looked like Seth and her heart squeezed.

After the wedding, McKenna would probably get pregnant. Then these gatherings would be three against one. Selena gulped. She'd really be the odd one out.

As if sensing Selena's discomfort, McKenna thumped one hand on the table. "Enough baby stuff. We're here to talk about the wedding. Do you believe Logan suggested a destination wedding?"

"But why?" Vanessa's forehead puckered. "I thought he had tons of friends in Chicago, since his grandmother still lives on the West Side."

"Apparently, that's the point. We want a small wedding but he grew up in River Forest. His grandmother has a lot of friends there who might be hurt if they aren't invited. If we go away for the wedding, Grandma Cecile won't have to deal with that problem."

McKenna had really taken to Logan's grandmother. Kind of like Selena had bonded with Seth's mother. Her fingers shredded a paper napkin into thin strips. Vanessa and Amy were tossing out names of cities. Traveling sure sounded good. Fewer Kirkpatrick friends at the ceremony to ask questions like, "Did you and Seth split up?"

Amy rapped on the table. "I'm all for a destination wedding. After all, a trip brought Mallory and me together. Right now, we could use a getaway vacation."

"That bad, huh?" Selena struggled to sound upbeat.

"We need to get away. We love Gianna to pieces but we're always together. My parents would jump at the chance to babysit. They're always complaining that they don't have enough time with her. Thank goodness Mallory bought that house in Oak Park."

"An understanding guy," McKenna threw in.

And loaded. That sure helped with the extra houses.

"Do you think everyone will be able to get away for a

destination wedding, McKenna?" Selena had her doubts. So many of their friends worked in healthcare.

"Logan and I talked about it. Of course Big Mike and Reenie will want to invite the entire Oak Park Fire Department, people from their church, the Garden Club, Rotary and every other organization they belong to. But we're serious about wanting a small wedding. At some point, we might have a party back here in Chicago. Do you think people will be insulted if they're not invited to the actual ceremony?" McKenna's brows drew together in a concerned frown.

Amy and Vanessa chimed in.

"Not at all."

"Do what *you* want."

McKenna and Logan were such a good couple. Selena had watched the attraction grow while they worked with women in the Guatemalan highlands.

Back then, she'd been dating Seth and she'd wanted the same happiness for McKenna. Lulled by the heat and humidity from all the rain, Selena had fallen asleep in her hammock every night dreaming of Seth. Scooping up another handful of peanuts, she crunched them in her fist.

McKenna's eyes had grown dreamy. "That trip was special for us. Seeing Logan work with people so different from his own privileged upbringing made me love him even more."

"What about Italy for the wedding?" Amy threw in. "Mallory and I found out first-hand how romantic Tuscany can be."

Laughter erupted. Amy's story was funny, now that everything had turned out. A high school teacher herself, she'd been engaged to a coach. The wedding was only two weeks out when she found her fiancé in the locker room shower with Greta, the gym teacher. The wedding was off but Amy wasn't going to give up her honeymoon. Selena admired her for that. An Internet site had paired her up with Mallory. But the female "museum aficionado" she'd hoped for turned out to be a man.

Incredible, terrifying and, in the end, so romantic.

One week and Mallory knew what he wanted.

The kind of story Selena wanted for herself.

Only that wasn't happening.

McKenna wrinkled her brow. "Italy is tempting. But it's a long flight."

"Won't any destination wedding involve travel?" Selena asked. Getting out of town would feel so good about now.

"Maybe. Let's order." McKenna passed the menus around. "Do we have to leave the country for a destination wedding?"

"Savannah's very romantic," Amy piped up. "Just ask your sister Harper about that."

"I'm open to that. And I think Logan would be too. After all, I went to Savannah for St. Patrick's Day that year Harper was working for Cameron. Beautiful city and they have weddings in Forsyth Park in the heart of Savannah."

"The splashing fountain, trees draped in Spanish moss…" Amy's face glowed. Although she had a home in Oak Park with Mallory, they lived in Savannah most of the year.

By this time, the menus had been forgotten and all three

women wore moony expressions. *Caramba.* Just what Selena needed. Friends dreaming about their men. Staring at the menu, she didn't see a word. The waiter arrived.

"Selena?" McKenna pointed to the menu. The waiter was looking at her with a question on his face and so were Amy and Vanessa.

Embarrassment singed her cheeks. "Oh, I'll have the burger." The others laughed and Selena felt like an idiot. After all, the Purple Frog only served burgers. Even the waiter was chuckling. With that curly blonde hair and blue eyes, he was adorable. In another lifetime, she would have flashed what Seth called her high-watt smile.

But this guy wasn't Seth. And that was the problem.

She met McKenna's eyes. "I'll have whatever you're having."

Nodding like she understood, McKenna gathered up the menus. "That'll be two Bacon Bacado Burgers. And plenty of those sweet potato fries, please." Amy and Vanessa both ordered, and the waiter left but not without a backward look.

"Oh, I think the boy has eyes for you, Selena," Amy teased.

The air had turned tense, the way a delivery could feel when the cord was unexpectedly wrapped around the baby's neck. In fact, Selena felt like she was choking and took a quick sip of water.

"Any other thoughts about a city for the wedding?" McKenna asked.

Time to join the party. "What about Santa Fe?" Selena suggested. "You feel like you're in another country but it's not that far away. My brother Rafael married Ana in the Loretto Chapel.

Beautiful ceremony. They live in Santa Fe now. Both teachers."

McKenna's eyes brightened. "Hey, I like it. Logan might go for that. What's the weather like in May?"

"Pleasant. Not any warmer than Savannah would be. The wisteria will be in bloom." The tension eased. The music changed to something by Sting that involved dolphin sounds. Soothing. Calm.

But when her phone pinged, Selena's shoulders tightened. She didn't have to look to know this was Seth. Again.

Turning, McKenna raised her brows. Apparently she'd heard the phone. Reaching into her pocket, Selena turned it off. Seth knew what he was doing to her and she wasn't going to let that happen.

One sniff of the burgers a few minutes later and Selena's appetite revived. "Did you cook these yourself?" She batted her eyes shamelessly at the cute waiter.

"Yeah, sure. Hope you like it. I can be pretty handy when I try." Slapping a towel over his shoulder, he grinned. Selena felt the other women exchanging glances.

"My, oh my. I'd like to see you try." The words felt strange. Her flirting skills needed a serious tune-up. Did he wink as he turned away? Her friends got busy with their burgers but she thought she heard Vanessa giggle.

"Was I bad?" Ravenous, she took a huge bite of her burger.

"Good to see you put it out there again, girlfriend," McKenna joked. "Lately you've been acting like you were married with none of the benefits."

Amy and Vanessa exchanged a glance. "Except sometimes there are no benefits, Selena," Vanessa said slowly. "Sometimes marriage is just doing the laundry, figuring out what's for dinner and getting up at night with the baby. Trust me, marriage isn't all roses."

Mouth full, Selena had no comeback. That all sounded great to her. But Team McKenna was carrying the ball. "Truth is, my knuckle-headed brother isn't stepping up to the plate. Selena's booting him out of her life and I totally understand, I guess."

"I'm so sorry." Amy's eyes brimmed. She was so darling and soft-hearted. "You make such a good couple."

"Honestly, I feel so stupid, Selena. Forget the lecture." Vanessa gave her head an impatient shake. "A girl's gotta do what she's gotta do. I know that."

"I'd personally like to kill him." McKenna's cheeks flushed. Nice to have Seth's sister on her side. "He should be coming through with some permanent plans."

"That's right."

"Absolutely."

Amy and Vanessa both agreed whole-heartedly.

Selena was dipping a sweet potato fry in the ketchup when she heard McKenna say, "Look, there's Gary." Gary Rice was Logan's partner in the OB Gyn practice at Montclair Hospital. "And he's with ... my, oh, my."

Their heads swiveled. Somehow Selena moved her jaws and swallowed. Then she trained her eyes on McKenna. "Did you have anything to do with this?"

"Just helping you along." McKenna met Selena's eyes directly.

"I was down in the ER consulting with Gary when Seth's crew brought in a patient. He may have overheard me mention we were coming here."

Okay, I can do this. I can get right in his face.

"We talked about this, remember?" McKenna dropped her voice. "Time to walk the talk, girlfriend."

Selena pushed her plate away. Across from her, Vanessa lifted eyes brimming with sympathy. "Oh Selena, I know how you feel. Sometimes I want to strangle Alex. He was so hardheaded about some things."

Amy nodded. "True love never runs smooth. Maybe it's that Mars and Venus thing."

Throwing her head back, McKenna gave one of her earthy chuckles. "Right. We come from opposite planets. But we are the sun, ladies. Let's remember that."

McKenna always kept things in perspective and Selena joined in the laughter. "Are they still there?" she later whispered to McKenna.

Looking in the direction of the bar, McKenna whispered back, "Yep. Let the games begin."

"You got that right." Whipping out her small mirror, Selena applied another coat of candy-apple red gloss. She feathered some of her bangs over one eye.

The waiter came back and they paid. She smiled broadly at him and he stumbled as he turned to go. McKenna, Amy and Vanessa got busy with their jackets. Sliding out of the booth, Selena pulled on her red quilted jacket and matching red and white striped stocking cap that accented her dark hair. The hat never did fit. Curls sprang out every which way.

"Let's form a line," Vanessa suggested. "You're in the middle." Giggling, the four of them snaked to the front of the bar like they were doing the bunny hop, hands on each other's waists. With Amy and Vanessa in front of her and McKenna warm against her back, Selena felt ready for whatever came her way.

While they giggled, Livvy Wright broke off from the Montclair group. Tossing back her long dark hair, she checked herself out in the mirror over the bar. Selena's breath tightened when the attractive nurse sauntered over to Seth and draped herself over his shoulder.

Exactly. And this happened all the time.

McKenna poked her in the back. "Keep moving."

Feeling like the top of her head might fly off, Selena stumbled forward.

The others had noticed. Even Vanessa and Amy were craning their necks and their steps slowed. Whatever Seth said to Livvy, her face turned the color of an August tomato and she flounced away. Back on track, the four of them barreled toward the bar, right into Seth's path. The moment of truth lay just ahead.

Broad shoulders hunched in a gray sweater she'd given him for Christmas, Seth was watching some game on TV. She doubted that he even knew the score. Sitting next to him, Gary pounded one fist on the bar. Were Seth's eyes ringed with dark circles? Amy and Vanessa waved hello just as McKenna pulled Selena to a halt.

"What are you guys doing here tonight?" McKenna stared

daggers at her brother. Selena almost burst into giggles. Seth sure didn't look happy, like he'd lost a patient in the ambulance. The couple of times that had happened, she'd comforted him until he realized it wasn't his fault. Her smile faded. Now she wanted to soothe that wrinkled brow and brighten the shadowed brown eyes that had lost their sparkle. They'd always been good about supporting each other in a field where losses happened and hearts broke.

But he'd lost the right to her comfort.

"Just stopped in for a drink." Gary's eyes swept the group. Clearly, Seth had clued him in about what was going on. Selena had heard that Gary and Mindy Muenich had broken up, and they'd dated a long time. Must be a lot of that going around. Post-holiday breakups. No one ended a relationship before Christmas. Just not in the spirit of the season.

January? Relationships lay scattered like discarded wrapping paper.

While she talked with Gary about a new piece of equipment, Selena could feel Seth's eyes on her. Her legs threatened to melt. Then McKenna poked her. That sharp elbow said *be strong* and Selena picked up the tempo. Tilting her head, she twisted a curl around her finger.

Ramping up her sassy attitude, she almost didn't feel the touch on her elbow. Startled, she glanced back into the eyes of the waiter she'd flirted with earlier.

"Hey, see you later?" With his adorable grin, he slid something into her pocket. Then he was gone. Flustered, she fingered the edge of a card. Seth looked like he might explode.

"See you guys later." McKenna led the way to the door. Gary waved good-bye but Seth stared at the bar, visibly seething. His square jaw shifted and his full lips compressed into a thin line. *Excelente.* Selena busted out of the Purple Frog feeling like she'd just finaled in the Olympics. Exhilarated by the cold night air, she was almost clear when she felt the tug on her jacket. She tried to pull away.

But Seth wasn't letting go.

Chapter 3

Seth gripped Selena's jacket tight, the way he did at a football game so they wouldn't get separated. Up ahead, McKenna turned back with a questioning look. The last thing Selena wanted was an audience and she shot her friend a thumbs-up. "I've got this," she mouthed. With a pleased smile, McKenna turned back to Amy and Vanessa. The three friends had scored parking spots along the street but Selena was in a parking garage.

Yanking her jacket from his hand, Selena spun into action. "What's up, Seth?"

"Nothing much. How about you?" Dropping his hold, Seth rammed his arms into his brown leather jacket. His fresh soapy smell washed over her. Her shiver had nothing to do with the frigid air. She locked her knees.

"You going to call that guy who gave you his card?" Seth's tight smile didn't reach his dark eyes. He might be playing it cool. But she could be cooler.

"That's none of your concern anymore, is it?" Tossing her head back, she hoped the streetlight made her dark curls shine.

His nostrils flared. "Don't you think you're being ridiculous?"

"Me? Never." Translation: *always.*

Looking cautious, Seth settled his hands on her shoulders. Not on her hips, which would be restricted territory. Not that she was overthinking this at all. "Babe, you can't be serious about Sissy. I was half asleep that morning."

"Yes, I know. You were dreaming. But not about me." Her voice cracked, like ice breaking underfoot.

"Aw, Selena, come on. I always dream about you. You know that." His eyes closed to a sexy slant, absurdly long lashes deepening them to hot chocolate.

"At least you could remember my name." Putting both hands against his chest, she pushed away.

Seth gave her a calculating look, like he was thinking about what to say next. Not too long ago she tried to teach him how to play chess but he didn't have the patience. This was the expression he'd worn during the chess game. They'd switched to checkers.

Puffy white flakes sifted from the sky, catching in Seth's gorgeous auburn hair. How Selena longed to brush the snow away and cup that square jaw in her hand. A stiff Chicago wind slapped some sense into her.

Looking at the man she loved, she longed for the certainty of crocus and lilacs. Instead, they stood on an icy street, curbs heaped with dirty snow. And doggone it, Seth looked totally lost.

The situation was enough to make a grown woman cry. But not her.

He fingered a curl that had escaped from her knit hat. "You always look so cute in this cap."

One touch and Selena's entire body went on melt alert.

She should wear this hat every day.

Or maybe she should never wear it again.

Get a grip, Selena.

When she didn't say anything, he jammed his hands back into his pockets. "Why aren't you answering my calls or texts?"

"Nothing to say, Seth."

He frowned. "But we always have a lot to say to each other, don't we?"

The man was clueless and badly in need of some Main Man training. A girl's Main Man would say things like, "I love you." Not, "What game do you want to watch tonight?"

"Maybe you're just not saying what I need to hear."

"Now, what would that be, babe?" Oh, oh. The hands were out again, kneading her shoulders. But honestly? She was tired of holding up cue cards.

"I think you know what I want to hear." She fought the urge to curl up in the arms she knew too well. Truth was, they talked plenty about the city's worsening traffic problem and global warming. They were always in step on those issues. But tonight the words she longed for were more up close and personal.

A light sparked deep in his eyes. His hands stilled. Maybe Seth Kirkpatrick wasn't totally clueless after all. "You know I care about you."

"Is that right? You 'care' about me?" Frustration spiraled through her body. His hands slid back into his pockets and the frown returned. Time to lay this out for him. "Care about me enough to go to bed with me but not enough to..."

Did she have to say it? Really?

Never in a million years. Backing away, Selena lost her footing on a patch of ice. Her boots slipped out from under her and her arms flailed.

In a heartbeat, Seth had her. He set her upright with gentle hands, like she was his mother's Belleek china. "You have to watch your step. It's slippery out here."

He always took care of her that way. Seth Kirkpatrick would shoulder his way through crowds ahead of her, open doors, walk on the outside of the sidewalk or hold an umbrella over her during a rainstorm. He made her feel like a sweet little thing when actually she'd grown up working in the fields alongside her family. But right now?

Their relationship was seriously stalled, like a Chicago L train with a mechanical problem. And Seth? He might never make it to the next station. Maybe it was time to face that.

"Drive safely, you hear?" He was backing away, hands spread like he didn't know what to do next. Frustration fried her mind. He'd leave, just like this?

"So where do we go from here?" She wasn't about to hide from him like some frightened chicken.

"You tell me."

Seth was making her crazy, working the corner of those lips with his teeth. She still loved him, but she was tired of being the only one using that word. "I think we should be friends." Her words settled over them like wet concrete.

"Friends! That's it?" His words exploded in the cold air. Like they were watching football and the other team had just scored.

"Seth, really. We've meant so much to each other." She dropped her voice to the hoarse whisper she knew massaged the boy to the bone. "I'm not mad at you. I'm just disappointed."

His jaw clenched. That was a word his mother Reenie used with her grandchildren. They both knew it. The kids shriveled when they heard it and Seth was doing that right now. Selena didn't want to rip off his *cojones* but she did want him to see the light.

"I don't get it. What is it that you want, Selena? We've shared everything together. I- I L—. We've had such good times. Best buddies, right?"

He'd almost said he loved her and her heart stuttered to a stop. "Seth, I want to be more than your football buddy, okay?"

"Does this have something to do with that ticking clock thing?" Confusion swam in his eyes.

"Maybe. I really don't know. But I'm not wasting any more time on you when I know how I feel." Her voice thickened. She had to stop before she embarrassed herself.

"You think you've wasted time with me?" His face emptied.

"Let's just say you're not giving me what I need."

"But I thought we were so close."

Were? He was putting them in the past? "We were. No one knows me the way you do." She would trust Seth with her life. But her heart? She was beginning to wonder. Another gust of frigid air blew from the lake and she cinched her jacket tighter. "No hard feelings. See you around. Wish you the best and all that."

Whirling around, she gave a little hand flip, squared her shoulders and walked away. Hardest thing she ever had to do. But she would not turn back, not until she got into the parking garage and didn't hear any footsteps behind her. She pivoted slowly, wind whistling through the cinder block structure.

The garage was dark and empty.

Fine. Her father had taught her to fish off the city piers on Lake Michigan, an outing that provided Sunday dinner. "Let the line play out, *hija mia*," he'd say, loosening the bamboo pole in her hands. "The fish will circle some more, *no*? Jiggle it a little. You will feel that tug if you wait. Then you reel it in very slowly."

Her papá was a wise man. Remembering that tension on the line, Selena smiled.

~.~

The phone woke her up. Selena pulled at her quilt, trying to shake off the weirdest dream she'd ever had. Curled up with Seth on his couch, she couldn't get a word in edgewise. Words erupted from his mouth and coiled into bubbles that floated in the air. But they weren't his words. No, the dialogue belonged to every hot actor she'd ever admired, from Clark Gable to Ryan Gosling. Mouth working, poor Seth looked horrified at what was pouring from his mouth. And she felt the same. Chuckling, she reached for the phone. "This is Selena."

"Selena, I think it's time." Pam Dunlop's voice quivered with excitement and Selena's pulse kicked up. The pretty blonde wasn't due for a week but a woman's body took its own course.

Within minutes, she'd pulled on her clothes and was in her car, parked near her apartment in Wrigleyville, named for the baseball stadium nearby. The hospital was just north of downtown so it would take her twenty minutes to get there if she didn't hit any snags. At three o'clock in the morning, traffic was light on the Dan Ryan. She made it to the hospital in record time.

Heading straight for her locker, she changed into scrubs, netted her hair and slipped on some paper booties. Pam and her husband Jeff had been taken directly to the water-birthing suite. Warm, humid air bathed Selena's skin when she pushed the door open. The music they'd chosen for the birth of their baby played in the background. Ambient beach sounds would soothe the young couple and welcome their son into the world. Pam smiled nervously as her husband helped her into the water and Selena took her vitals.

It didn't take long for Selena to become caught up in the process that she loved more than anything. Joining McKenna in the For Women practice had been a thrill that never grew old. What could be more satisfying than bringing new life into the world?

Since this was Pam's second child, the birthing went as planned and James McCormick Dunlop entered the world squalling by five o'clock. Watching the father cuddle his wife and new baby, Selena felt her heart twist. For the past two years, she'd deluded herself into thinking that this would be Seth and herself one day.

What can a woman do when the man isn't ready?

The pediatric nurse began to go through the routine checks with the baby and after delivering the afterbirth, Selena and Jeff helped Pam onto the gurney that would take her up to the OB floor. Headed by Logan and McKenna, Montclair had been working on a plan to transform the obstetrics floor into an innovative labor, delivery, recovery and postpartum area. No more shuffling new mothers from one area to another. Selena had been so excited when the board voted to support it. And if she were honest, she pictured bringing her own baby into the world in that new unit, Seth by her side.

But she couldn't think about that now.

The nurse came to take mother and baby up to the unit and Selena shut down the water birthing room. The music was the last thing she turned off and for a second she let the sound of summer waves wash over her. *Madre di Dios,* she needed some warmth. Maybe she'd take off the rest of the day. The winter had been long and cold in Chicago, and the talk with Seth the night before had left her shaken. And then there was that dream. She shivered.

But who was she kidding? She had patients scheduled that day.

Ripping off her mask, hairnet and booties, she stashed them in the trash and hiked to the overpass connecting to the medical office building. Dorothy, their receptionist, was at the front desk but the lights were low in the waiting area.

"So you had a delivery this morning?" Dorothy turned on her computer.

"Yep, Pam Dunlop had a healthy baby boy." Selena's eyes wandered to their Wall of Fame, where pictures of their babies were posted.

"That's nice." Dorothy began to take messages from the phone system. "McKenna's in the back."

When she reached McKenna's door, Selena stuck her head in.

"Good meeting last night. Did you have a chance to run Santa Fe past Logan?"

Eyes sparkling, McKenna glanced up from her desk. "Yep, and he's all for it. His grandmother took him to Santa Fe when he was in high school. Logan thinks it will be a great place to celebrate our anniversary." Her greenish eyes turned dreamy.

"A man who thinks ahead and understands what it means to be close, really close." Selena choked. Her trips to Key West with Seth were their only travels together. He was a beach and ballgame kind of guy and his athletic bent suited her. She loved nothing more than a game of volleyball in the sand. But now she was searching for some commitment and the love behind those feelings.

McKenna was frowning. "Has Seth ever sent you roses, brought you candy?"

Slumping in the doorway, Selena nodded. "Hmm. Not really. A bunch of daisies one time." Frivolous things like that weren't in her family history. You can't eat flowers and sweets caused dental problems which they could not afford.

"My dad's not big on that kind of stuff either." The frustrated sigh from McKenna could have made a cloud scud across the wintry sky. "So, did you two have a good talk last night?"

"Not really. I don't think he gets it, McKenna. He doesn't think I'm serious about not seeing him anymore."

McKenna pushed back from her desk and Selena slumped into a wing chair. "Sometimes I think my brother avoids the difficult truths."

"Could be. Although I love your mother dearly, she spoils

Seth."

"You think?" The peal of surprised laughter made Selena get up and close the door. No need to bring Dorothy back here.

"I have brothers, so I guess I understand. Maybe all mothers prefer their sons, hope of the future and all that nonsense."

McKenna snorted. "Trust me, none of your brothers turned out like Seth. You come from good stock."

"Families don't come any stronger than the Kirkpatricks. Look at the firemen in your family, starting with your dad. Your family chooses to serve the community. But it was different for mine and I know that's hard for you to picture. I could never explain this to Seth. Nothing came free for us. *Nada.* All those years as migrant workers, my family had to be strong. Just smile and do the work. Back in Juarez, things were getting worse and we all wanted to stay here in this country. My parents were so relieved to be granted citizenship."

"Didn't you go to school on a state program?"

"Sure did. Made me appreciate all the things you Kirkpatricks take for granted."

"Have you told Seth all this?" McKenna's forehead wrinkled.

"Not really. It's so personal." She shook her head. "Not romantic at all."

Her friend snorted. "You two don't have a casual relationship, Selena. Seth isn't the type of guy to dig deeper unless you give him cause. Long ago, he told me you and your family had worked on a farm."

"That's about what I told him." Selena shrank into herself. Was she dishonoring her family, dismissing those long days and the back breaking work? "Oh, McKenna, *amiga mia*, I like being Seth's hot chili pepper. That's what he calls me." Just hearing her own words made her smile, brought back the times he'd used it teasingly with her. "What is it you say in this country about 'spilling your stomach'?"

"Spilling your guts," McKenna supplied.

"Right. That's about as pretty as it sounds. I don't want to bombard Seth with my family history."

"I think you have to risk some sharing. That's what couples do, right?"

Her friend became quiet and Selena felt uncomfortable. "What is it, McKenna?"

"I don't like to tell other people's stories but I think you know this. Seth hasn't been to college. You know that right?"

Selena shrugged. "Sure. *No importa*. He explained he wanted to be where the action is, an EMT, not sitting at a desk. So what?"

"Do you think sometimes that gets to Seth? The fact that you have more formal education?"

"*Caramba*, it never occurred to me." The thought horrified her on so many levels. "That's so crazy."

McKenna tossed a paper clip into her drawer. "Forget I mentioned it. Seth's pretty comfortable in his own skin. But growing up, he was never Connor."

"He's a good man in his own right." For her, Seth was nothing but confident.

Eyes distant, McKenna nodded. "Seth's hardworking. He's

charming but he'd never cheat on you. Still..."

"The women always have an eye for him." The incident with Livvy at the Purple Frog was still on Selena's mind. And it would only get worse when the word got out that they'd split up. Anxiety twisted in her stomach.

"Even as a baby in the grocery cart, Seth batted his long lashes at the ladies. My mother has stories."

Their laughter eased the tension.

"A chick magnet. Great. But I knew that when we started to date." Outside the wind wailed and the sky resembled flat sheet rock. "How I wish spring would come."

Looking out the window at the snow that had begun to fall again, McKenna grimaced. "Going to be a while before we see anything green around here."

Getting up and walking to the window, Selena rested her fingertips on the cold glass. "I don't know if I'm ever going to warm up. At least you have your wedding to plan."

"Why don't you get away for a few days? Maybe you and Seth need a time out. You know, the way my brothers do with their kids. Mark or Malcolm often warn them with "I want you to think about the consequences."

Selena smiled. She'd heard the guys say that.

"Meanwhile," McKenna continued, "have some fun. Show Seth what the consequences might be. There are plenty of single men right here in this hospital."

"Name one." Weren't all the single guys at Montclair dating someone?

"Gary and Mindy decided to call it quits."

"So I heard. Do you know what the problem was?"

McKenna shrugged. "Guys never talk about stuff like that. Logan just mentioned that Gary was bummed out so maybe the breakup wasn't his decision. Trust me, he's a keeper. If not for Logan, I may have made a move on Gary."

Wow, *que sorpresa.* "Now the truth comes out."

"Just a thought at the time. We women have to keep our options open." Checking the clock on the wall, McKenna gave a stretch. "Full patient load today and Bethany's sick. That leaves two midwives and a full schedule."

"Got it." Selena sprang up to leave.

But before she pulled open the door, McKenna gave her a big hug. "Ever been to Savannah?"

"No. Why do you ask?"

McKenna wore a mysterious smile. "Maybe you should visit Harper for a couple of days after Bethany gets back. In Savannah, the sun shines most of the time. Might give you the break you need. Help with the time out."

Selena's spirits lifted. "You sure Harper wouldn't mind?"

"She'd love it. You could tell her all about our planning session. She hated the fact that she couldn't fly up for our meeting at the Purple Frog. Cameron's restoration business has a lot going on right now. But she'll have time for you. She can tell you all about why she dumped Billy. Not that Seth is in any way as bad as Harper's former boyfriend."

"Mick Jensen's wedding is coming up. Seth and I were

supposed to go together, so I'd sure like to be gone for that."

"Perfect time to get out of town." McKenna grinned.

"You got that right." Leaving the office, Selena made tracks of her own. Time to pick up the pace. No way was she going to sit around Chicago if she could help it.

Although the day continued gray, after her talk with McKenna Selena felt hopeful. McKenna gave Harper a call and all systems were go. By the end of the day, Selena had a plan. She'd always had a good relationship with McKenna's younger sister. As far as the flights went, the closest dates turned out to be around Valentine's Day weekend, the same weekend of the wedding Selena wanted to avoid. "That all right with you?" she asked Harper when they talked.

"Any time's fine with us. Cameron loves to have people around. I think he was talking about a family dinner for Valentine's Day. You can join us. It'll be fun."

It felt so good to have plans. Being single after two years of being part of a couple didn't feel great. Dating Seth, Selena had always been busy with hockey, basketball or football games. How she would miss the Sunday dinners with the Kirkpatricks. Although McKenna encouraged her to continue to come, Selena just didn't have it in her heart.

This time she had her own plan and it didn't include Seth Kirkpatrick.

Maybe Savannah would give her just the change she needed, although she'd be with Seth's sister. How would that work?

Chapter 4

Selena's connecting flight had been delayed in Atlanta. By the time she trudged up the ramp at Savannah, it was almost two o'clock in the afternoon. Her empty stomach growled and her head ached from all the caffeine. But she felt hopeful. Outside, the sun was shining. The sight of Harper beaming at the top of the ramp made Selena giddy. McKenna's sister had been an art student and the girl was a walking parade in an orange sweater and green pants. Harper smelled like spring, all fresh and flowery, when Selena hugged her. "Sorry my flight's late."

"No problem. I had a cup of coffee and relaxed. We've been so busy renovating a house in the Victorian District, and Cameron said I needed some down time." She exhaled with a happy smile. Her brilliant Kirkpatrick hair spilling from an orange and green head scarf, Harper looked glorious. Maybe that's what love did for a woman.

When it was returned, that is.

"I think Savannah really agrees with you." Catching sight of herself in a gift shop window, Selena wondered when she'd picked up the deep circles under her own eyes.

"You mean Cameron agrees with me, right?"

"Must be. I met him at Christmas and he sure seemed like a

great guy. I'm happy for you."

"Yeah. He is." From the expression on her face, Harper had drifted off to dreamland.

Dragging her carry-on over the stone courtyard, Selena blamed the tension in her neck on Seth. She'd run into him twice in the ER over the past two weeks. Would she feel better or worse if she didn't see him and went cold turkey? His texts were dropping off. She felt both relieved and disappointed.

Good Lord, she was a hot mess.

The cool Savannah air, which would feel like spring in Chicago, bathed her cheeks when they pushed outside but the sun blinded her. Had she even brought her sunglasses? Tipping her face up, Selena closed her eyes and for one blissful moment just felt the heat. Not much sun that winter in Chicago.

In the courtyard outside the airport, bright red canna lilies skirted the walkway. A fine mist fell over them as they passed the splashing fountain between the parking structure and the airport. Every muscle in Selena's body started to unwind. "Why is it that everything always looks better when you're in another town?" She looked around with wonder.

"Isn't that the truth?" Harper took her arm. "As much as I love Cameron, sometimes I miss my hometown. I'm so glad you could come."

"Thanks for inviting me, although I think McKenna took care of that."

"You bring a breath of fresh air from the Midwest."

"A cold breath, although I do love Chicago. You know, the

bustle of a big city." Or had Seth taught her to appreciate his hometown? He'd taken her to all the ball games, Buckingham Fountain and even the zoo.

Delete. Delete. She was going to enjoy her time here, not wallow in memories.

When they entered the coolness of the parking garage, Harper led her to a black SUV. "Most of your family still in Michigan?" Clicking her remote, Harper popped open the trunk and Selena swung her bag inside.

"My parents settled in Kalamazoo, and two of my brothers and my younger sister live there too. McKenna may have mentioned that Rafael, my oldest brother, married a girl from Santa Fe. He teaches high school out there and so does his wife Ana. " She slid into the passenger seat next to Harper.

"I hear that's where we'll be for McKenna's wedding. I'm excited and so is Cameron." Harper snapped her seatbelt shut and Selena did the same. In no time, they'd exited the parking garage.

Taking in the greenery by the side of the road, Selena smiled. "Palm trees? Are you kidding me?"

Harper gave her a sideways glance. "McKenna said you're having a rough time right now."

"You could call it that."

"My brother's not easy."

"Sometimes I wonder if I'm expecting too much." Had Selena ever heard her father tell her mother that he loved her? Those signs of affection weren't common when she was growing up. But her parents did have a partnership with shared goals. Did she have that with Seth? They'd never sketched out a future together.

As they passed a huge sign for the Airstream Corporation, Harper gave her a glance that reminded her of McKenna. "I guess that's up to you, Selena. What do you want from a man?"

"Good question. Part of me wants to be a career woman. I love my midwifery work with McKenna and the years of training weren't easy. I'm not about to walk away from all that."

Harper broke into a chortle. "That will never be you, Selena. Besides, can't a woman be married and still work, even after the kids? I doubt that McKenna will give up her career after she marries Logan. What's your plan?"

Selena's throat tightened. "We never got to that part. I would love to be married and still work, at least part-time. But I don't know if Seth feels that way. Just never came up."

They'd come to a stoplight and Harper hit the brake hard. Selena jerked forward, seatbelt tight across her chest.

"Sorry, Selena. Are you kidding me? Seth never talks about marriage? He's crazy about you."

The pleased heat bathing Selena's face felt almost embarrassing. "Is he? Really?"

The light changed to green and Harper pulled away. "Whenever I get him on the phone, all he does is talk about you."

"He does?" She tried to squelch the hope fluttering in her heart.

"Absolutely. I ask him how he's doing, what his next step is. But all he does is talk about the latest pair of twins you've delivered or a difficult breech birth. He's so proud of you."

"Next step for Seth? What do you mean?"

"Oh, you know. He's an emergency tech but shouldn't he be taking classes to be a paramedic? After all, he's almost thirty. Seems like he should be moving on with his career in emergency medicine. He thrives on it."

By this time they'd turned onto Hwy 95 and the only sound was the hum of the tires. Sitting silent, Selena mulled over Harper's words. Had she been so self-centered that she'd never even considered that the man she loved hadn't worked out his career goals? "Oh, *Díos mío*," she groaned.

"What? Don't you think Seth should continue his education, while he's still working? From my experience, getting a degree doesn't ensure a job. My family supported me through college, and Seth was part of that. I was grateful not to have a loan when I graduated here in Savannah. But I felt so stupid not having a job after everything my family had done for me. Cameron helped me put all that together. Takes a little work. Couldn't Seth take the classes at night?"

"Of course he could." Selena's voice sounded as hollow as she felt. "I never asked him about this. Where was my head?" She felt terrible.

Reaching over, Harper squeezed Selena's hand. "Now, don't go blaming yourself. Seth's a big boy. This should be his decision."

"Yes, but we should have talked this over, I guess."

Harper snorted. "Sure. Right. Like a Kirkpatrick man is going to allow that. Look at Connor and Amanda. From what I understand, he never admitted that becoming a father terrified him. Five years trying to become a dad and they never covered that topic?"

Propping an elbow against the closed widow, Selena rested her head on one hand. "I feel so stupid."

"Don't blame yourself. This has to be Seth's choice."

"Right. And loving me has to be his decision too."

"Of course he loves you. He might not know how to say it. The boy's never been good with words." Harper glanced over and the SUV bobbled.

"Watch the road, okay, Harper? You're making me nervous." But Harper's words bothered Selena more than her driving.

"Sorry." Harper refocused her attention on the road ahead but her forehead stayed puckered. "You mean my brother's never even told you that he loves you? How long have you been dating?"

"Two years," Selena said on a defeated sigh. "And no. No he hasn't. We have no plans."

"Wow." Amazement echoed in Harper's voice. "What's going on with him?"

"Not your problem. As you said, Seth's a big boy." Selena didn't want this mini-vacation to become a painful therapy session with Seth's sister. That wasn't fair to Harper. Besides, Selena had come here to forget. "So what should we do while I'm here? Although really, I can find my way around by myself." She was plenty good at doing that.

"Don't be silly. You're giving me an excuse to ditch work. And I've got the boss's approval. There's a lot to see in Savannah. I might just wear you out. Cameron and Bella can't wait to see you. Connie, Cameron's housekeeper for years, is picking Bella up today from school. They should be home when we get there."

"How does it feel now that you're a girlfriend and not just the nanny?" Bella, Cameron's little girl, had been a difficult child with an eating problem.

"Feels amazing, my own Cinderella story come true. Of course, relating to kids is something that comes with time and it's never easy. Just ask Amanda. When I saw her at Christmas time after they brought Sean home, it was like I was looking at a different woman. Babies and toddlers take a lot out of you. Bella was a little older. No night feedings, just that attitude."

Selena chuckled. "Kids are never easy." But she was so ready. Her heart and soul clamored for *bebés*. Seth's babies. But she wasn't here to think about him. Time to concentrate on the gorgeous scenery and count the palm trees. By this time they were in the city, headed for the house she'd heard so much about. Doing a mental sweep, Selena tried to clear her mind and leave any worry about Seth behind. When Harper pulled into the garage behind a mansion that would put Tara to shame, Selena's eyes almost dropped out of her head. "Are you kidding me?"

She'd never seen anything like this, *una casa grande*. Sure there were houses like these on the west side of Chicago. In fact, McKenna had mentioned that Logan's grandmother lived in one in River Forest. But Cameron's home had a certain southern grace. Maybe it was the side garden with the fountain. Or the wisteria climbing the wrought iron railings of the double balconies. And that wasn't all. Lots of boy toys were parked in the spacious garage. They scooted past a red Porsche and a black auto with classic lines.

"His Bentley." Harper pointed to the stately car as they exited through a side door. The sun filtered through the tall oak trees as Selena dragged her suitcase over the mossy stones in the garden.

Harper led the way. "Really is something, isn't it? When I came here for my job interview, I almost turned around and left. Sure wasn't Oak Park, and I didn't know if I could handle it."

"I see what you mean." Hadn't Selena felt that way so many times in her life as she struggled to change from the girl who worked in the fields to the girl who went to college? The sunlight and beautiful plants in the courtyard, along with the mermaid fountain, began to melt the block of ice in her chest. "Your sister was right. Coming here was a great idea."

"The magnolias and the palm trees stay in bloom all year round. The live oaks lose their leaves but you really don't notice it because of the moss draped on their heavy branches. And we rarely have snow." Harper grinned. "That's sure a plus."

Selena followed Harper up the back stairs, almost hating to leave the beautiful courtyard behind. This peace and serenity were why she'd come. Maybe she'd have time to relax in this garden. Harper pushed open the oversized back door and sang out, "Connie, we're home!"

A little girl with a mop of dark hair dashed from a side room, a huge brown dog galloping at her heels. The girl skidded to a sudden halt but the dog kept coming. In no time at all, Selena was given a thorough licking by a quivering ball of fur. She liked pets, although growing up they'd never had any. Feeding the children was hard enough for her parents as they followed the crops from farm to farm. Migrant workers rarely had pets.

"Selena, I'd like you to meet Bella and Pipsqueak." Harper laughed as she hugged the spirited little girl.

"Pipsqueak! Stop that." Taking hold of the dog's collar, Bella frowned. Looking chastened, the dog sat down, his pink tongue lolling from his mouth.

"Cameron took Pipsqueak to obedience school," Harper murmured from the corner of her mouth. "Worked great, right?" Meanwhile, Bella studied Selena. The little girl was a charmer. Her pink top set off her dark hair. The bright scarf? Looked like Harper was rubbing off on her little charge.

"Hi, Bella." Bending forward, Selena put both hands on her knees. "Remember me from Christmas? I met you at the party at Kirkpatricks' house."

The little girl nodded, eyes flitting between Harper and Selena like a little humming bird. Although she slid two fingers into her mouth, one frown from Harper and both hands disappeared behind her back.

"Can you say hello to Selena?" Harper urged her.

"Hi, Selena. Are we going to get ice cream?" Bella's question made short work of her shyness, as if the words had been running through her mind all morning.

Harper rolled her eyes. "Okay, I may have mentioned that we plan on going down to Leopold's for ice cream while you're here. Bella's not about to let me forget that promise."

An older woman bustled into the kitchen, smoothing back pale blonde, frizzy curls. An enormous apron was wrapped around her ample waist. Harper introduced her. "Connie runs the place." The housekeeper blushed but obviously they had a good relationship.

"I can see you have your job cut out for you, Connie." The large kitchen held an impressive collection of copper pots hanging over an enormous stove. The aroma of coffee and some kind of soup wafted through the air. The housekeeper reminded Selena of Seth's mom. Wearing a quiet air of authority, she was clearly queen of the kitchen.

Edging toward a doorway, Harper said, "I'm going to get Selena settled upstairs. Her plane was late."

"Take her to the room your sister used when she visited last year. Everything's ready," Connie told her.

McKenna had visited Savannah to cheer Harper up the year before. At the time, Harper had been having some trouble with her new position and of course, McKenna snapped her out of it. Selena had been given all the colorful details, which had made her own trip here doubly appealing. Maybe this time Harper could be the one to provide help. Her comments about Seth had sure given Selena a lot to think about.

Harper led the way from the kitchen, Bella trailing behind with Pipsqueak, the dog's paws clattering on the white marble floor. The enormous wainscoted foyer held heavy carved pieces and stone-topped surfaces on what looked like priceless antiques.

"This place is huge," Selena's voice echoed against the vaulted ceiling.

"I know. The first time I sat on this bench my stomach was doing cartwheels." Harper motioned to a hand-carved bench and they began to climb the stairs. When they reached an upstairs landing, Selena couldn't tear her eyes from the large paintings lining the walls.

"Don't be too impressed," Harper whispered with a saucy grin. "Cameron picked up the furniture at the Bull Street auction, even the portraits. Trust me, that is not his family."

Selena had no clue what that meant but it made her smile. Maybe things never were as they appeared.

"Want to see my room?" Bella wiggled in between them.

Harper smoothed back the little girl's hair—a natural gesture that tugged at Selena's heart. McKenna's little sister had always been on the wild side. Maybe she'd left those days far behind. "Why don't we leave that for later, okay? Selena's probably tired."

But Selena hated to see Bella's smile droop. "I'd love to see your room, Bella." Face brightening, Bella led Selena into a room that was pure magic. So many toys. Such a magnificent bed. Selena couldn't help thinking about the cramped migrant worker housing from her earlier years. Her mother had worked to keep the one or two rooms as clean as possible. But they were never in one place for long. Toys? Selena could only recall a Raggedy Ann doll that she'd passed down to her younger sister Sofia. Her mother had to replace the black button eyes at least twice.

In Bella's room, the dolls and toys sparkled like new and the high four-poster bed was fit for a princess. "You are one lucky girl."

"Harper decorated the room for my birthday last summer." Taking Harper's hand, Bella gazed up at her with adoring eyes. That look tied a knot in Selena's throat. Harper had found her place in the world while Selena felt like a kite bobbing aimlessly in the air.

Selena looked up to find Harper's eyes on her. "Um, why don't we show Selena her room, Bella, and let her get settled?"

The climb to the third floor reminded Selena that she hadn't gotten much sleep the night before. Her legs felt shaky by the time they reached the spacious landing. Harper turned into a bedroom with long windows that overlooked the street. The walls, coverlet and curtains were green—pretty but dated in a charming way. Americans were always so quick to replace older household goods and clothing that remained useful. Selena could never understand it. Her family liked the old ways, where pots, quilts and family stories were passed from one generation to the next.

Weariness rolled over her and Selena stifled a yawn. The broad, high bed sure looked comfortable. She'd gotten up in pre-dawn darkness to catch her flight. Harper opened the empty top drawer of a white bureau. "Just don't leave anything behind. When Connie was showing me my room after I signed on as nanny, she found a hot pink thong from the last nanny."

"I didn't bring any," Selena said when she stopped laughing. "Figured I didn't need one this weekend."

"Good to know." Harper closed the drawer and pointed to the doorway. "Bathroom's in the hall with a clawfoot tub to die for. See you downstairs when you're ready?" Harper gave her a quick hug. "So glad you're here, Selena. Now, take your time, okay?"

"Sounds good. I won't be long."

The dog sniffed at her heels, probably curious.

"Come on, Pipsqueak." Bella called from the stairway. The dog hesitated but soon disappeared. After zipping open her carryon, Selena arranged the few clothes she'd brought in the drawer. Harper's story about Connie had left her with an idea, a plan of action for a hot chili pepper. But that would have to wait until she got back to Chicago. Now the bed looked so tempting, the springs creaking *un poco* under her weight.

This bed would have been too soft for Seth.

The thought gave her satisfaction because this trip was only for her. As she closed her eyes, Pipsqueak settled at her side. The warm bundle reminded her she was someplace else and that felt good.

Chapter 5

The wet lips on her cheek made Selena smile. "Seth, *cariño*. Let me sleep a little more, *por favor.*"

Then it all came back. She opened her eyes. Tail slapping the white coverlet, Pipsqueak offered another affectionate slurp. "What the heck?" Groggy, she pulled herself up.

Late afternoon sunlight fell through the window and somewhere nearby traffic hummed. Visiting Savannah and sleeping? No way. Jumping up, she found the bathroom and splashed water on her face. Her dark curls were snarled and she ran a long-tooth comb through them and dashed on some lipstick before heading for the stairs. Pipsqueak nearly tripped her in his excitement. Once on the first floor, she followed the sounds of voices back to the kitchen and found Harper studying recipes with Connie. Intergalactic battles crashed on the TV screen in the family room, where Bella was watching cartoons.

"Have a good nap?" Harper looked up with a smile.

"I am so sorry. Didn't mean to punk out on you."

Barreling into the kitchen to join the party, Bella tugged on Selena's jean jacket. "Want to go to the park?"

"She means Forsyth Park downtown," Harper explained. "We could do some exploring. It's still midafternoon."

Selena smiled down at Bella. "Know what? I would love it if you would show me Forsyth Park." The little girl beamed back. How lucky Harper was to have this little sweetheart in her life.

Bending down, Bella scratched Pipsqueak behind his silky ears. "You be a good boy for Connie now, you hear?" Pressing a damp nose against Bella's cheek, the dog gave her a sloppy lick.

Lulled by contentment, Selena felt her disappointment and heartache ease just a little. The kitchen was filled with the smell of bread baking, and the sun streamed through the tall windows. Winter had been banished and didn't this lighter jacket feel good? Harper showed her a couple of recipes she'd been considering.

Harper and recipes? The whole thing felt surreal.

How comforting, to be caught up in the everyday rhythms of a home filled with love.

When Selena first moved to Chicago, her apartment quickly became a refuge. After the crowded rooms of her past, she'd never wanted a roommate. The space of her three room apartment in Wrigleyville felt luxurious. With so few possessions, she hardly knew what to put in the closet or her private storage space in the basement. She painted the walls, strung curtains and bought her first big screen TV. Living alone felt private and peaceful.

Then she met Seth. Her whole life changed. The two of them talked about living together, but the conversations were casual. Time passed and that didn't happen. Sleepovers? Sure but moving in together posed problems. He lived near his job and she lived near hers.

Maybe the distance between them was just another sign this was never meant to be. Her younger sister Sofia talked a lot about *buena suerte*. Either you had good luck or you didn't. But in Selena's book, people made their own luck. Her parents had taught them this.

"Are we ready to ride?' Harper broke into Selena's thoughts by clapping her hands. Bella ran to grab a jacket.

"Have a good time," Connie called out as they exited the kitchen.

Outside, fifty-five degrees felt a lot better than the twenty degrees back home. Selena cast a lingering glance at the courtyard. Maybe later. Within minutes they were in the car, Bella secured in her carseat in the back.

Instead of taking the parkway downtown, Harper chose Abercorn. "The street runs through town so you'll get a real feel for it." As she drove, she pointed out the various areas.

"These trees!" Abercorn was shaded by huge live oaks, dripping with moss that seemed to almost touch the cars. The frozen streets of Chicago faded from her mind. She was here to forget. Finally they reached Forsyth Park, the longest park Selena had ever seen. It took a while to find a parking space so Harper drove around the green expanse, giving Selena a chance to see more. The gorgeous fountain shone through the shadows under the huge trees. Finally a parking space opened up and Harper wedged the SUV into a space near a band shell.

Unsnapping her own belt, Bella waited eagerly in the back seat until Harper scooped her out. Arms wind-milling, the little girl ran toward the other children. "I don't need you to push me on the swings. Just watch."

"We'll be sitting right on this bench, okay Bella?" Harper called after the rambunctious little girl. Bella joined a clutch of children waiting their turn.

"Hard to believe she can pump herself on those swings. But I'm all for it." Harper settled onto a bench between the play area and the beautiful fountain Selena had seen in more than one travel photo.

And to think she was here. She took a seat next to Harper. "This is so gorgeous. It'll be a while before they turn on Buckingham Fountain in Chicago."

Carefree travelers snapped selfies in front of the gargoyles and water sprites that were part of the iconic Savannah fountain. While Harper kept her eyes on Bella, Selena took in the scenery.

"What a nice life you have here, Harper, so carefree and cozy."

Harper's glance veered back to her, but only for a second. Bella was clearly her main concern. "Wasn't always this way. Things started out pretty rocky. Bella was a handful and so was her father. I can't tell you how many times I wanted to throw in the towel and head back to Chicago."

Lips pulled to one side, she shook her head. "Back then, procrastination was my middle name. I'd gone through so many jobs after graduation. When Cameron took me on as a nanny, I became determined to see this through, especially after I met Bella. Then I had to stick with it."

"And in the end you got the guy. You created your own good luck."

"Guess so but it wasn't easy. I'd been dumped by my long-term boyfriend Billy. Nothing was going right. But this position..." She nodded toward Bella, pumping like crazy on one of the swings. "I wouldn't let myself fail. She needed me."

"McKenna said Bella had a feeding problem at the beginning?"

"Right. And she's still a little squeamish about some food, but she's put that behind her. I'm really proud of her."

"You sound so motherly, Harper."

Harper smiled mysteriously. "Amazing, right?"

"Do you want children of your own some day?" Stupid question to ask a Kirkpatrick.

"Yeah, I sure do. How about you?"

"If I can give them a good life, of course." No crowded bedrooms with mattresses on the floor for her. Selena's stomach twisted at the thought. "I have mixed feelings about child care."

"Did you have a lot of babysitters when you were growing up?"

The warmth in Harper's eyes eased open a door Selena had closed firmly behind her. "Harper, I grew up in the migrant worker camps. That's how my family survived. It wasn't unusual for my parents to take us with them to the field during the day or a packing plant at night. They had no choice."

"Oh, Selena. Honey, I never knew."

Maybe this was a day for leaving past hurts behind. "My youngest brother, Domingo, died from exposure to fertilizers. He was only two. My mother was never the same."

Harper's green eyes deepened to river stones. Why had Selena brought this up now? The Kirkpatrick family and the Ruiz family were as different as night and day. "I'm sorry, Harper. I never should have mentioned..."

The carefree screeches of the playing children were probably all Harper knew—a life of swing sets, tidy classrooms and the same smiling teacher the entire year.

"Selena, I always knew you were a tough cookie. Seth never mentioned any of this. Wait a minute. Does he know?"

Stomach shifting, Selena didn't want to ruin this beautiful day by talking about the past. "It's not exactly date conversation, Harper."

"Seth is more than a date, Selena. You two have been together for a while. Why are you holding back? It wasn't until I learned about Cameron's family life that I knew I could love him." Harper's cheeks flamed, another Kirkpatrick trait. "At least, if the relationship is serious, a couple should have no secrets."

Secrets? "Oh, but I wasn't holding back on purpose..."

"But Seth would want to know this. He'd never think less of you, Selena, trust me. I know my brother that well."

Had she blocked Seth out? Selena wanted to forget her past but to be truly close to a man, she might have to share it.

Harper's words settled over Selena like the fertilizer she'd feared as a child. Her throat swelled until it was hard to swallow. "When did you become so wise, Harper?"

The bright sun bounced off Harper's curls when she shook her head. "Oh, no. Not me. You're the smart one, Selena. And you'll come through this. But you have to lift the veil, right?"

"Maybe I'm just too proud to tell him what it was really like for me growing up. He knows I went to school on grants and so did my entire family. He never asked any questions."

"Probably never occurred to him. And I'm not saying this is why he hasn't moved your relationship along. I just know that meeting Cameron's family helped me understand him better. It made me love him more."

Selena was speechless. Harper had given her so much to think about.

"My brother can be a total idiot sometimes. I don't know why Connor and Mark can't slap some sense into him. They both got married and wanted a family, pretty much the norm. "

"Maybe that's not on Seth's agenda. Hard to say what's normal." Selena had tremendous respect for other people's choices.

"For most people. I hate to see you suffer because of my stupid brother. He sure kept us laughing when we were growing up. Connor was so serious about being the oldest in the family. But Seth? He was always cracking jokes."

Memories flooded Selena's mind. One Halloween they went to a costume party with Seth dressed as a tube of toothpaste and she was the brush. "You can squeeze me any time tonight," he'd whispered, always lots of fun. And underneath that, chemistry off the charts.

Dates with Seth were like that...one glance, one comment and they both had the same thing in mind.

But a marriage had to be more than that. More than just physical.

Harper considered her with those hazel eyes that could turn moss green, just like McKenna's. "A husband has to be a partner in every way, Selena. I think that's Seth but I'm beginning to wonder."

Selena gulped and sucked in the humid Savannah air. Time to put on her big girl pants. "I'm at decision-making time, Harper."

Suddenly Bella left the children and dashed toward them. "Hey!" she called out before hurtling into Harper's arms. "Can I get some loving?"

The last was delivered in the sweetest tone. Harper's arms closed around Bella and tears swelled in Selena's eyes. A tight hug and Bella was gone.

"That's new." Harper shook her head, smiling. "I think she saw it on TV."

"Adorable. Maybe we should all ask for what we want."

"Wish life were that simple." Seth's baby sister reached over and squeezed Selena's hand. "You'll do the right thing."

Plans were formulating in Selena's head. She was going to help Seth do the right thing too. The boy would never know what hit him.

"Bella, take your turn," Harper called out. Standing in line for the slide, Bella bobbed up and down like a jumping jack. The kid had ants in her pants, as Seth's mother would say. "Maybe I'm lucky that Cameron had been single for a while. He had time to date after his wife passed away."

Selena had heard the sad story of Tammy, Bella's mother, killed in a tragic accident when Bella was only two. Life could be so unfair.

Jumping up, Harper stretched. "I should ask Bella if she has to use the restroom. She always forgets when she's playing."

"Okay, I'll wait here." Taking out her phone, Selena checked her text messages. A warm shimmer ran over her skin. That surge of excitement every time something popped up from Seth made her crazy. These must have come in while she napped with her phone off.

Stopped at the hospital today. Looks like you're MIA. Miss you.

Twenty minutes later. *McKenna says you're on vacation. Glad to hear it.*

That one made her chuckle. Was McKenna poking the bear? But it felt good to hear from Seth.

Just when she thought he'd forgotten her.

Number three. *Weather's crummy here. Where are you anyway?*

He still felt he had the right to ask? Selena snorted so loud that a passing woman glanced over. A rogue breeze sent the fountain spray her way, the droplets chilling Selena. He was so very wrong. She flipped to the next message.

I'm thinking about you. Hope you're thinking about me too. Love ya.

Crazy thing about her boyfriend, well her ex-boyfriend. He could add that to any of his messages. "Love, Seth." But he couldn't say those words to her directly.

She had to stay in his face. Her fingers flew. The phone should have caught fire from the comments she typed in. Told him just how warm the day felt on her skin and other parts of her body. How amazing that smoke didn't pour from the small keyboard.

Finally, she jammed the phone back into her shoulder bag with a pleased smile. Tipping her face to the sun, she tried to get back in the zone. What a wonderful day. The sound of splashing water reminded her she was far from Chicago, away from the man who drove her crazy. And now the shoe was on the other foot. She flexed her bare toes in her sandals. Time for a pedicure.

When Harper and Bella returned from the restroom, the three of them left the park and walked up along Bull Street, where jewelry and gift items sparkled in the windows.

"Can I have a new purse, Harper?" Bell pressed her nose to a window where beaded evening bags glittered.

"You don't even use a purse yet." Harper tugged a length of Bella's dark hair playfully. "What would you put in it?"

Lips pursed, Bella thought about it. "My phone?"

"You don't have a phone."

Mischief sparkled in Bella's eyes. "You could get me one."

"You are a minx, you know that?" Harper led Bella away from the window.

The youngster's nose wrinkled. "What's a mink?"

Selena almost busted out laughing.

"The word is minx and it means stinker. That's you." Harper touched a forefinger to Bella's freckled nose.

Instead of being insulted, Bella looked pleased. The two were such a natural pair. Of course they had a future together, although Cameron and Harper weren't engaged. Yet.

Was Selena expecting too much from Seth? Uncertainty gnawed at her along with Harper's comments. Had she been keeping things from Seth? Would that really affect their relationship? Not watching where she was going, Selena tripped but Harper's quick save kept her from falling.

"You have to watch these cobblestones. They've been here for ages and the roots of the trees have pushed them up." Harper glanced at the time on her phone. "We should probably head back now. Cameron will be coming home."

The soft glow on Harper's face when she mentioned Cameron's name made Selena turn away. Toes throbbing from her near fall, she followed Harper to the car. Once upon a time she carried that happy glow because of Seth and maybe she still did. The man had his good points. No matter how hard she battled those memories on the way back to the mansion, they wove through her mind like the Spanish moss hanging from the trees overhead.

"Cameron has plans for us tonight," Harper told her as they pulled into the garage. "Nothing fancy but he's taking us out for dinner. In fact, he's taking us out tomorrow night too for Valentine's Day."

"Oh, boy." Bella's eyes were as big as the huge hibiscus in the garden. "Me too?"

"Yes, you too. That okay with you, Selena? Cameron asked his mom to come in for Valentine's Day. Kind of a family gathering." Harper paused. "You're practically family, at least in my book."

That old odd-woman out feeling surfaced again, no matter how hard Selena tried to beat it back. "I feel like I'm crashing your party, but thank you for including me." Last year she'd spent Valentine's Day with Seth and they'd gone to one of Chicago's fine Italian restaurants. This year she probably would have been home watching a Netflix film with a quart of chocolate chip ice cream she definitely didn't need.

"We're glad to have you." Getting out of the SUV, Harper opened the back door and Bella climbed out.

"Yay! We are going out for dinner," Bella echoed in a sing-song voice. After everything she'd heard about Bella's feeding disorder, Selena was delighted by the little girl's excitement. Eager to shake her funk, she grabbed Bella's hand and together they skipped through the side yard.

A little while later, the yapping of the dog announced Cameron's arrival. Selena and Harper were talking quietly in the kitchen and Connie had left for the day. Scrambling from the sofa, Bella scurried from the TV room and threw herself at her father's legs when he came through the back door.

"Some day, you're going to knock me right over." Cameron swung Bella up into his arms. Was there anything as sexy as a dad caring about his child?

"Oh, Daddy." Bella tucked her head under her father's chin.

Stooping, Cameron gave Harper a kiss. "Miss me?"

"Always. Say hi to Selena."

Cameron had to tear his eyes away from Harper. They were so *preciosa* together. "Hey Selena. Did you have a rough trip?"

"Not at all. And we had a great afternoon at Forsyth Park."

Cupping her small hands on either side of Cameron's face, Bella said, "Daddy, I saw the prettiest purses in the store today. Can I have one?"

Cameron and Harper shared a glance. Like two parents. Like partners.

"What are you going to put in that purse, darlin'?" Cameron's attention circled back to his daughter.

"A phone?" Bella squeaked out. "Harper said so."

"Oh she did, did she?" Cameron gave Harper a glance that could melt marble.

Giggling, Harper wagged a finger at Bella. "I did not. You better explain." What fun they had together.

"We can talk about this another time." Cameron put Bella down. "Don't want to be late for our reservation at Pearl's. Who feels like some hush puppies?"

"Me, me! I want some!" While Bella clapped, Pipsqueak danced around the kitchen, barking the entire time. Selena rushed upstairs to freshen up and change into her black pants and quilted jacket over an animal print top. By the time she made it downstairs again, Cameron and Harper were both wearing jeans and sweaters.

"We love Pearl's because we get to watch the sunset over the marsh," Harper told her as they drove down Victory Parkway.

Selena was seated in back next to Bella. "Will we see pelicans tonight?" Bella piped up.

"I asked for a table at the window," Cameron said.

Sure enough, when they were seated at a window table for four, two pelicans were perched on the dock that wrapped around the restaurant. "Oh my goodness," Selena sighed and sat back. "How peaceful."

"High tide." Cameron nodded at the water lapping the marshes below. "If the tide were lower, you'd see a lot of gray mud and crabs scuttling around."

"Ew, Daddy. Yuck." Bella pressed both hands to her mouth.

"Sorry, sweetie, but you know it's true."

Selena loved Lake Michigan but the marshes had a wild beauty.

"Not a bad seat in the house is there?"

Harper's eyes swept the view with obvious appreciation. "We come here pretty often. Bella enjoys it and the food is really good."

The waitress brought their menus.

Selena found out a lot that night. Her first discovery was that she loved hush puppies served with honey butter. Looking totally pleased with herself, Bella split one of the small balls open and did a pretty good job slathering it with the topping. Both Cameron and Harper seemed to hold their breath but Bella began to nibble. Their trepidation was no doubt an old habit that might take time to break. From what Selena understood, the little girl hadn't eaten anything but cereal until she was four. That had been Harper's greatest challenge.

Selena took her time with the menu and was very happy with her choice. The cashew encrusted mahi-mahi tasted fabulous but the interaction at the table was what interested her most. Here was a couple who'd both had their problems, and yet they'd put them aside to come together. Harper's boyfriend had taken off for California, and she was wondering if she should even stay in Savannah when she signed on as the widower's employee. Cameron was at his wit's end. So many nannies had quit on him. Chuckling, he admitted he'd hired Harper for her Chicago spunk.

"So are you taking your trip to Guatemala this summer?" Cameron asked after the waitress had brought key lime pie for dessert.

The question brought Selena back to the realities of her own life. "Yep. Not sure about McKenna and Logan, but Gary Price might go, one of the other OBs."

"You do such good work there." Harper nibbled on the graham cracker crust of her pie. "All those women need your help."

"They appreciate us and the group of clinical volunteers grows larger every year. At least one physician comes to help with the more difficult cases that require surgery. "

"That is so cool." Picking up her napkin, Harper wiped Bella's chin. The little girl had ordered ice cream and quite a bit ended up on her pink top.

"Am I doing good, Daddy?" She looked to her father for approval.

Cameron nodded. "You're doing great."

"Excellent," Harper threw in. "I'm proud of you, Bella."

They had all the markings of a family. The three looked to each other for approval and laughed over shared experiences. Yep, these three were naturals.

She would have that one day. Picking up her fork, she cut off a huge mouthful of key lime wonderfulness. Staring out over the water, she considered all kinds of options to try with Seth. Her afternoon texts had caused a sand storm of return messages. She was saving them to read later.

"Tomorrow night we're going to another restaurant I think you'll enjoy," Cameron announced. "It's Valentine's Day and I think you ladies need a night out."

And watch them make eyes at each other? A good book

sounded better. "Why don't you let me babysit?" Selena offered. "You two could have a romantic evening."

Bella's lower lip came out. "You mean, I wouldn't get to come?"

"Thank you, Selena." Cameron quietly intervened. "But we promised Bella. My mother's coming in with my sister and we're making an evening of it. Is that all right with you?"

"Absolutely. Look forward to meeting them." She was glad she'd escaped Chicago and it was only right to go along with whatever Harper and Cameron had planned.

"Grandma's coming? Is it going to be a party? Like my birthday?" Bella asked, voice high with excitement.

"Your birthday was in May, Pipsqueak."

"Daddy." Such disdain in the voice. "Pipsqueak is our dog."

Throwing his head back, Cameron unleashed a gutsy laugh that turned heads.

"We know that, Bella." Harper threw Cameron a look that made him press his napkin firmly against his lips. "But you were the first Pipsqueak, remember?"

Blushing, Bella whispered in her nasal voice, "Sure I remember, Harper. But then I growed up."

Another family discussion ensued. The long day had Selena's eyes flagging. By the time they drove home she was more than ready for bed. "Wonderful day. See you in the morning." She gave Harper a big hug at the foot of the stairs.

"How about some sightseeing tomorrow?" Harper suggested. "Cameron offered to spend the day with Bella. My Valentine present."

"Sounds good." Anything to keep her body and her mind busy. Climbing the stairs to the third floor, Selena flipped open her phone and laughed softly at Seth's first message. Uh, huh. The boy was getting frisky.

And there were so many more texts to enjoy later in bed.

Chapter 6

Seth watched Mick and Maria circle the dance floor in the roving spotlight. Another high school friend married off. Mick's parents looked like they'd died and gone to heaven.

Holding the phone wouldn't make it ring so Seth put it away. The texts from Selena today made him wonder how he ever wound up here alone. The guy with the mic invited the wedding guests to join the happy bride and groom. Seth slouched down in the metal folding chair, glad for the bushy pink flowers on the table. How many single men were left in his crowd? Not many.

Taking his phone back out, he read Selena's last message.

He missed her like crazy. Why had she gone to see Harper?

After all, *he'd* never been to Savannah. Seemed strange and it bothered him. His own sister. The trip felt disloyal.

Just then Sissy Hanson drifted past with champagne and a giddy smile. "You expecting a call, Seth?" Leaning over, she offered an ample view of her low neckline. Subtlety wasn't her strong suit.

Keeping his eyes straight ahead, Seth jammed his phone back in the pocket of his monkey suit. He'd been a groomsman in Mick's wedding. If this kept up, he might as well buy a tux. "Thought I felt a vibration. Friday night and all."

"Really? I've been having such a great time visiting...maybe I should check my phone too." With a knowing smile, Sissy snapped open her handbag. Why did women always bring those itty bitty bags to weddings? Staring down at her phone, Sissy frowned. "Nope. No calls. Guess we're in the same boat."

No way. "Easy mistake. That band is so loud." By this time, other couples had joined the bride and groom on the dance floor.

"Where's Selena tonight?"

Sissy must not have gotten the memo yet about the breakup. "Out of town."

"Hmm." Snapping her bag closed, she leaned closer. "Well, since you're here, want to dance?"

Right. Sissy would post an innocent but incriminating photo on Facebook. All hope of winning Selena back would go down the drain. "Think my brother is waving to me, so I'll have to pass. Excuse me, Sissy."

After all, this was the woman who had gotten him into trouble, although she didn't know it and certainly wasn't to blame. Across the floor, Connor was holding court and Seth headed his way, sidestepping the dancers. Last thing he wanted to watch was couples slow dancing, whispering in each other's ears. Since their parents were babysitting for Sean and they liked to turn in early, he suspected Connor and Amanda wouldn't be here long.

Before he reached their table, the music ended and an announcer grabbed the mic. "All right now, all the single men on the dance floor. Could be your lucky night, fellows." Doing a quick about face, Seth veered toward the exit. He could talk to his brother tomorrow.

Out in the dark parking lot, two overhead lights glinted off the tops of cars. A February wind swept North Avenue and he headed to the far corner where he'd parked. Shivering, he popped open his trunk to pull out his heavy jacket. At first he thought the sound he heard was the wind. Slamming his trunk shut, he stood there for a second, cold air whistling round his head.

The pathetic wail came again, faint and needy. Searching the darkness, he saw movement next to a dumpster in the back. "Anybody there?" Could be a lost child. You just never know. As he stepped toward the dumpster, a patch of gray flattened itself against the metal.

What the heck? An animal out here at night? Crouching, Seth held out a hand and wiggled his fingers. Better to let the poor thing come to him. No need to get bitten by a frightened animal. "Come on, now. Bet you're hungry, right?"

But the mass of gray fluff that crept out shyly to sniff his outstretched hand was anything but dangerous. Barely filling his hand when he scooped it up, the poor kitten was starving, its skeletal frame puncturing his heart. "Where did you come from, huh? Were you born under someone's porch? Did you lose your mama?"

Climbing into his car, Seth blasted the heat. The kitten shivered in his lap. "I'm going to get you home and find you something to eat." He had no idea what he had in his kitchen but he sure wasn't going to leave the kitten out here to die.

~~

Comfy in the bed, Selena tapped on her messages. The dinner with

Cameron and Harper had left her feeling lonely. Those two were just so comfortable and lovey with each other. Her resolve began to melt. Missing Seth like crazy, she dug into his messages like they were key lime pie.

Friday night and I'm stuck at this stupid wedding without you. I'd rather be somewhere private, just the two of us.

So the wedding was stupid? She tapped the phone against her lips. Usually they stopped at the Purple Frog on Fridays for a burger. Sometimes they even drove over to the Comeback Inn in Seth's neighborhood. Besides the peanut shells on the floor and the yummy aroma of their grilled burgers, Comeback had a moose head hanging above the roaring fireplace. The back half greeted visitors on the other side of the wall.

Sigh. History. She missed it. She missed *them* as a couple.

She clicked on the next message.

Don't you miss your hunky hottie, mi amor?

No fair giving her the sweet talk she'd taught him.

Mi amor? Seth was more like *mi problema.*

And she had no solution.

Why aren't you here to dance with me?

She could picture Seth surrounded by old friends, every girl hoping to catch his eye now that he was a free man. And that boy knew how to dance. He could put Channing Tatum to shame with his sexy moves.

Her fingers got busy. *Know what I miss?*

Typing away, she named a few things to get Seth's pulse racing. She laughed, picturing how uncomfortable he might become, and in public too.

But it had been a big day. Plugging the phone into her charger, she turned out the light. She'd come to Savannah to get away from Seth. What was the point if she kept thinking about him? When she was still wide awake thirty minutes later, she blamed the key lime pie. Grabbing a *Southern Life* magazine from the basket next to the bed, she settled in to read until her eyes finally flagged.

~~

"Did you sleep okay?" Harper asked Saturday morning when Selena joined her for coffee in the kitchen. Bella was watching TV and Cameron had already left to visit one of his project sites.

"Like a baby," she lied. No sense having Harper think this visit wasn't appreciated. "When I woke up, I couldn't remember where I was. Then it hit me. Savannah, city of sunshine." Seth had been her next thought. He'd sent her a Happy Valentine's text. Of course it was a joke, not the mushy kind she would have liked.

"Want to go shopping? Clothes? Shoes? What's your pleasure? Cameron will be back in thirty minutes and he wants us to have a girls' day."

"All of the above." Anything to keep busy.

By the time Cameron returned, they were ready. The Truman Expressway wasn't very crowded as they headed downtown. The sun was shining and she was going to explore a new city.

"Thought we'd start at a market area. Lots of shops and great food." Harper pulled into a parking garage.

"Sounds wonderful."

About two blocks from the river, City Market bustled with

tourists. Selena picked up an aqua T-shirt with Savannah emblazoned on the front. The shirt would always bring back this day, she hoped, and the feeling of her new found freedom. Maybe she'd do more traveling.

But that sure felt like running away.

Since Harper was into art, Selena followed her through some of the galleries but nothing really caught her eye. Although Selena liked art, she seldom bought any. Today she wondered why. Her work paid well enough to allow indulgences. What was she waiting for?

Her own home. With her own husband.

When Selena tripped, Harper grabbed her.

"I'm fine. Just a crack in the sidewalk."

"Got to watch where you're going," Harper warned her. "These cobblestone walks are older than we are. Old and mean." They both laughed. The uneven pavement wasn't totally to blame for Selena's stumbling. Sometimes a sudden realization can make a woman careless.

Her life was on hold. Like a plane waiting to land, she was circling. Waiting for a house. Waiting for a husband who would decorate the house with her. Since when had waiting been her style? Maybe she should start creating that home herself.

She pulled her attention to the store windows. In one of the art galleries, she saw a beautiful flock of what looked like gulls taking to the sky. The artist had rendered the birds in some shiny metal. The piece lifted her spirits. "What do you think of this, Harper?"

Standing back, Harper contemplated the striking piece that

seemed to lift right off the red brick wall. "I love it. So beautiful and free. Does it remind you of Lake Michigan? Cameron and I don't go to Tybee Island that often so I don't see gulls much."

Selena chuckled. "Somehow I can't see this in Cameron's home. All the history in that mansion calls for historical paintings, like the guys with the handle-bar moustaches in his parlor."

"Sometimes that's a problem." Harper frowned.

"Really? That gorgeous mansion is a problem?"

"Believe it or not, yes. Cameron's been married and he's had the house for a while. Everything is pretty much the way he likes it. But design management was my major in college, so I'm itching to make my own mark on the house. I mean, when it's appropriate." Her voice faded and her cheeks flushed. The rosy glow made Harper even more beautiful.

"So what's the future for you two?" Selena had to ask. "Not that I'm prying but I am curious. Do you have plans?"

"No details yet." Harper's eyes turned a misty green. "I mean, I just can't imagine my life without Cameron and Bella. I really can't."

The girl was in serious need of a hug and Selena obliged. "You probably won't have to even think about that. I'm the one concerned about my future." Her eyes drifted back to the gulls, so darned inspiring and totally impractical.

She made up her mind. No more waiting. "This piece is perfect for my bedroom wall. I want to wake up every morning, looking at these birds soaring into the sky. I want to feel this in my heart."

"You go, girl. You'll figure all this out. Seth is not about to let you get away. Count on it."

"Maybe I need a reminder of who I am hanging on my wall."
Selena pulled out her wallet.

After buying the piece and making delivery plans, they walked
back to a little French bistro called Goose Feathers that served the
most delicious breakfast sandwiches ever. "The food here is
fabulous," Selena murmured, sipping her lemonade between bites
of egg, croissant and sausage.

"It's impossible to diet in this town." Harper reached for the
sticky bun she'd ordered. "Want to split this?"

"Bring it on. No way am I counting calories on this trip."

When they finished eating, Harper and Selena strolled onto
Broughton Street, thick with college students and tourists. Sun
warm on her shoulders, Selena was so glad she'd come. The change
of scene made her feel like her old self, the woman she used to be
before she met Seth. How had she ever allowed a man to have so
much power? But Seth didn't take it. No, she'd given it up. Most
weekends she waited to see what his plans were. How crazy was
that? From now on, she would set her own schedule.

Shopping had never been high on her list. Just wasn't her thing
with the midwifery business keeping her busy at all hours. But
being here with Harper in an exciting city got Selena in a shopping
mood.

Passing a shoe store, she took stock of the window display. "I
could use some walking shoes."

"Globe Shoes is one of the best shops in town, but not for
walking shoes." Harper's eyes danced. "The shoes in this store?

For kicking up your heels, girlfriend." They went inside.

Selena had the best intentions. But she threw walking shoes aside to study a pair of black boots with tiny covered buttons that would sculpt a woman's calf perfectly. Her legs had always been a point of pride. She practically salivated.

Harper followed her glance. "Going to try those on?"

"You better believe it."

While she pivoted in front of the floor mirror, she pictured Seth's reaction to the sexy boots. Twenty minutes later, she left the store with a sizeable box. The boots? She might wear them on the plane.

Farther down the street, she found a pair of walking shoes and Harper bought a cinnamon colored sweater that set off her hair. When they reached a tea room, of course they stopped. Although tea had never been Selena's thing, the blueberry scones were to die for. Stomachs full, they wandered through a furniture store specializing in modern furniture with long, low sofas, enormous coffee tables and floor lamps in geometric designs. Selena would never see anything like these in her parents' modest home. But they were very happy with their three bedroom split level in Kalamazoo, with a traditional high-backed sofa and comfortable overstuffed chairs. They moved on.

The card store had a sale on valentines. Selena hesitated while Harper snapped them up. "To tuck away," she told Selena with a smile. "I'm big on sales."

Buying mushy cards for next year would be trusting in the future. Selena was through with that. But when she flipped open a musical card that played the chicken dance, she had to have it. Even if she only played it for herself, the card was worth it.

Then they hit Leopold's, the iconic ice cream shop that she discovered still made chocolate sodas the old fashioned way, thick and syrupy. She ordered hers with coconut ice cream while Harper decided on a chocolate malt. Selena insisted on treating her. Kirkpatricks always liked to pay their own way so it wasn't easy to snatch the check from the fresh-faced boy at the counter. Harper grabbed for it. But her hostess soon relented, leading the way to one of the old fashioned marble-topped tables. Selena slid into a bentwood chair.

"I've probably gained three pounds today." Scooping up a spoonful of whipped cream, she studied it and smiled. "Not that I care."

"Calories don't count on weekends or vacations," Harper reminded her between hearty sips of her malt.

Chocolate soda rich in her mouth, Selena nodded. "I'm with you on that. So what's Cameron's family like? I'm looking forward to meeting his mother and his sister."

Harper took a second to think about that. Sometimes she reminded Selena so much of Seth. "They're not what you expect. Think I'll leave it at that. Cameron comes from a small town a couple hours outside Savannah. He really gets along with his sister Lily but the mother? Not so much. His dad died last year and I went to the funeral with him to watch Bella. The two of them had never gotten along. Very weird vibes."

"At least Bella has grandparents."

"Right, and Tammy's parents are still in town. Cameron makes sure that Bella sees them, although it wasn't always that way. Of course, adults love Bella. She charmed Big Mike and Reenie when we came home for Christmas."

Christmas seemed so long ago. The holiday had felt warm and cozy with Seth. The chocolate soda chilled Selena's mouth, suddenly hard to swallow so she stopped. She let the ice cream melt in her mouth. When they drove up to Kalamazoo, Michigan, to visit her parents over the holidays, her mother had gotten her alone for a minute and asked her about the future. Selena didn't have an answer. Her mom had married very young, often a necessity in Juarez, so it was hard to explain where she was with Seth. Feeling strangely protective, she didn't want her family to think less of him because they had no plans.

In his later years, her father had taken a job in a nursery, while her mother worked in the reception area of a hospital. They saved up and bought a home in Kalamazoo. Rarely talking about the past, the entire family focused on the future. Clearly her mother saw Selena's future with Seth.

Her soda glass was empty and she blotted her lips.

"Time to head back?" Harper glanced at her phone and smiled. "Just a note from Cameron."

Yes, Selena wanted to be that girl, telling Seth all about this shopping trip. Despite all the fun she'd had with Harper, she was uncomfortable about the evening. For the last two years, she'd spent Valentine's Day with Seth. Those memories weighed on her heart.

Grabbing her bags, she followed Harper out of Leopold's. She would not check her phone today. That was about as hard as trying not to scratch her chicken pox years ago. The walk down Broughton felt long, but Selena's heavy bags made her happy. Finally they reached the parking garage near City Market.

When they got home, Bella was waiting for them in the kitchen. "You should've taken me," she said, lips puckering.

"This was big girls' day, okay?" Harper ruffled Bella's hair and the rueful smile dissolved.

"Hey, you're home." Looking comfortable and casual in jeans and a gray T-shirt, Cameron came into the kitchen and kissed Harper's forehead.

Selena headed for the staircase. "Think I'll go put my new clothes away."

"Can I come, Selena? Pretty please?" Leaving Harper's side, Bella turned toward Selena, hands clasped and pleading. The little girl could be a real drama queen.

Peering out the back door, Cameron held up a hand. "Wait a minute. Bella, I think your grandmother's here, along with Aunt Lily."

In the confusion that followed, Selena made her escape. With plenty of time to meet Cameron's family later, she took the stairs to the third floor two at a time. When she reached the bedroom, she threw herself onto the high queen-size bed and checked her phone. Sure enough, there were two more texts from Seth.

As if they were still together.

Stopped in at my folks today. They both asked about you. Said to say hi.

So he hadn't told them? And of course McKenna would never tell other people's news. She was as far from being a gossip as anyone could get.

Early in the afternoon another text had come.

Wanted to wish you a happy Valentine's Day in person. Bad. So bad.

He was bad. Bad to the bone and every pore in her body wanted him. She longed to feel Seth's lips, his warm breath, his strong arms. Head aching and heart sore, she drew a bath in the claw foot tub. After tossing in some lavender epsom salt from the linen closet, she turned on an old radio and sank into the steamy water. Smelled good and felt wonderful. Twenty minutes later, her body was totally relaxed but her heart ached.

She missed him.

What was she going to do about it?

Chapter 7

A knock came on the door.

"Selena? Everything all right in there?" Harper sounded concerned.

"Absolutely. Just unwinding." She couldn't remember the last time she'd fallen asleep in a tub, if ever. The bath water had cooled.

"Cameron has a reservation so we should hustle."

"Got it. Down in a second." Harper's footstep receded and Selena could hear barking and voices from below. Pulling the drain plug, she grabbed a fluffy white bath towel. Back in her room, she pulled on black leopard skin tights with a leather mini-skirt and a black quilted jacket over a lavender turtle neck. Time to show off her killer boots with the tights and short skirt. A few dashes of makeup and she was ready. Most people wore red on St. Valentine's Day but she was in a purple mood. The hammered gold hoops would be a great contrast to her shoulder length curls.

She wished Seth could see her.

The steps were kind of steep and she kept one hand on the railing going downstairs. When she drew close to the kitchen, the voices grew louder.

"Selena come and meet Cameron's mom and sister," Harper called to her from the TV room.

Harper had been right about Cameron's family. Selena never would have put these three together. The straight-faced older woman with iron gray hair sat alongside a younger woman who was her clone. No one would ever think these two were related to dapper Cameron. In between them sat Bella in a pretty red dress with black tights. Swinging her legs, she looked very pleased to be with her grandmother and aunt.

Harper motioned to the women. "This is Cameron's sister Lily and his mother, Wanda Blodgett."

"So glad to meet you." When the two women each shook Selena's hand, their palms felt work-hardened, like Selena's mother's hands. Wanda's eyes were glued to Selena's mini skirt.

"Selena is a friend from Chicago," Harper explained.

Not *my brother's girlfriend.* Just a friend. Well, she'd get used to it.

Cameron jumped up from the leather chair. "Guess we should hit the road. We have a private room but they won't hold it for more than fifteen minutes."

"A private room?" Harper echoed, looking gorgeous in a red mini-dress and black tights. Her heels with the dainty ankle straps must have come from Globe's.

"Yes, thought it might be nice. Special." He adjusted his red tie. "There's a shop along with the restaurant. Maybe you'd like to look around if we have to wait for our table."

"I don't really need anything," Cameron's mother said, hands folded across her purse.

"We just can look, Mom." Maybe Lily always acted as a buffer for her mother.

With a group this size, they took two vehicles. Cameron drove his mother and sister, and Bella wanted to ride with them. Selena climbed in with Harper.

"So what do you think of Cameron's mom?" Harper asked when they were about a block away from the house.

"Not quite what I expected, but no one ever is."

"Cameron's family helped me connect the dots. I understood him better."

Selena turned that over in her mind. "You're right. You can enjoy being with a man, feel physically attracted to him but long term? The family can seal the deal or be a deal breaker."

"Maybe you can love someone before recognizing it." Obviously Harper was still processing her words. "You know, without realizing that the feeling is love."

"How did you get so smart?" Selena teased while Harper turned red.

"Do you love my brother? I mean, I'm guessing you do. Just slap me if I'm being too personal."

"Loved him the first time I saw him. I had no reservations and maybe no common sense." One beat of silence and they both dissolved into laughter.

"But you know I love your family," Selena continued. "For me, the Kirkpatricks were the deal maker."

"And Seth? Does he like your family?"

"I think so. We're not together all that much." So far Seth didn't seem to have reservations about her family, even though he didn't know the whole story.

When they followed Cameron's car into the parking lot of what looked like an old, repurposed school, things promised to get interesting. They both got out and Selena studied the brick building that was definitely from a different time.

"I know this place looks weird but wait 'til you get inside. It reeks of charm," Harper told her.

Bella chattered from the minute she got out of the car. Taking his little girl by the hand, Cameron led the way, careful to help his mother up the steps. Seth was the same way with Reenie, although Cameron had a grand style all his own.

"Very cool." Inside the renovated school, Selena couldn't stop staring. The stunning gray decor was accented with chairs in orangey brown cordovan. The place smelled of leather, rich and warm. Working in a hospital, Selena was accustomed to a very different antiseptic smell. Cameron stepped over to talk to the receptionist while Harper led his mother and Lily down the corridor that led to the shops.

But Selena was shopped out. Growing up, they lived on a strict budget and it wasn't until she graduated from nursing school and made her own money that she began to buy things she really didn't need. It took a while before "impulse buying" became part of her vocabulary.

"Will you look at this old stuff?" Selena heard Wanda Blodgett mumble to her daughter. Used iron pans hung from the wall along with other antique kitchen utensils. Original artwork was displayed on another. Bed linens and woven blankets were folded on low tables. Ropes held monogrammed towels. Shops that had once been classrooms opened up on either side of the long hallway. Cameron's mother and sister disappeared into one.

Harper gave Bella strict instructions. "Don't touch anything."

So hard to do. This was a place set up to be touched with tons of stuff all over—lamps made of driftwood, buckets full of clamshells, napkins in every color, as if paper napkins weren't enough. The series of shops screamed "budget breaker." While Cameron's family ambled down the hall, Harper came back to where Selena was admiring some egg coddlers. She certainly never had time to do anything that fancy. Besides, Seth liked his eggs fried, sunny side up.

Would Selena ever use any of these frivolous things to outfit her home? Somehow she doubted it. She had her basic pan set and mixing bowls. Her favorite utensil was her *molcajete*, the mortar and pestle used to make guacamole. Good sturdy stuff–that's what her mother had used.

The shops gave her a whole new appreciation for the kitchen. With things the way they were, maybe Selena should buy her own house. Then she'd have a reason to use all these things. When she first met Seth and learned he was a bachelor with his own house, she thought he was planning for the future. In time, she began to suspect it was a continual project he enjoyed.

Her ears were attuned to the sound of the phone vibrating and she could hear it now, insistent and seductive. She resisted the urge to see who was calling. When Cameron's seating alert buzzed, he shepherded them back toward the restaurant, where a waitress showed them to a long, narrow private room.

Wanda Blodgett took it in with wonder. "Pretty fancy. Candles, huh?"

"Never seen anything like it," Wanda's daughter agreed. The wall was made of rough-hewn logs that jutted out to hold creamy candles glowing in the dimly-lit room. Like the walls, the table was a burled plank with tall chairs covered in cordovan leather.

The menu proved to be as unusual as the environment with root beer-braised short ribs and crispy squared flounder. The low country offerings made Selena's mouth water. Eyes roving the room, Bella looked awestruck and silent.

"And what is it you do in Chicago?" Lily asked Selena after the waitress had taken their orders.

"I'm in a midwifery practice with Harper's sister, McKenna. We specialize in water birth." Her career usually proved to be a conversation starter and tonight was no exception. Questions kept coming and she loved to talk about her work. When the first course arrived, conversation stopped and with good reason.

Selena started with a wonderful low country chowder and then went to the flounder. Bella seemed content with chicken fingers and sweet potato fries. Harper hovered over the youngster as if she were her own. From time to time, Selena caught Cameron giving Harper a glance that could have melted every one of the candles on the wall.

This was probably the most unusual Valentine's Day Selena could have but that was all right. Sometimes it's good to be with people you don't know that well. Cameron's family wouldn't ask her how she felt. Wouldn't feel sorry for her because she wasn't with Seth tonight.

While the conversation flowed around her, Selena felt pleased with herself. Wearing her new boots and looking pretty kickass, she was doing just fine without Seth. By the time they reached the chocolate mousse dessert with cinnamon hearts sprinkled in the dark swirls decorating the saucer, she almost believed it. The waiter served coffee and she was listening to Wanda and Lily talk about Hazel Hurst, their hometown, when Cameron tapped on his water glass.

As if they were at a wedding reception.

Then it hit her. She just knew. Excitement and horror knotted in her throat.

"I'm glad that families can be with us tonight, both my family—" and then he turned to Selena, who felt faint, "—and Selena, who's standing in for the Kirkpatricks."

Now, that was a stretch but she wasn't about to say anything to spoil this moment.

Harper's face paled when Cameron took a tiny blue box from his pocket. "I want witnesses tonight. I want everyone, both our families, to know how much I love you, Harper. How much I want you in my life always. Will you marry me?"

With a soft gasp, Harper pressed shaking fingers to her lips. The few freckles sprinkled across her nose darkened as she paled.

Bella's head swiveled between her father and Harper, who looked close to crying. "Say yes, Harper. Say yes, okay? What's in the box, Daddy?"

Cameron flipped the box open. The biggest rock Selena had

ever seen winked against the velvet inside.

"Oh, Cameron. Yes." Harper struggled to her feet. Her left hand shook when she extended it so he could slide the lovely solitaire onto her finger. Then he kissed her with such tenderness that Selena wanted to sob. The moment was magical. The way it should be, although proposals rarely are. Family and friends...wasn't that what marriage was all about? Cameron took Harper in his arms as if she were the most precious thing in the world. Yes, this was just the way it should be.

Selena joined Wanda and Lily in light applause.

Bella settled back, her eyes still on the box. "Can I have that box, Daddy. Can I?"

His handsome features creased into a smile. "You'll have to ask Harper, darlin'."

While the waiters brought coffee, Harper dialed her parents. Selena could hear Big Mike roar, "It's about time."

The rest of the evening was a blur. The longing in Selena's heart felt almost painful, she missed Seth so much. That proposal was what she wanted.

Forgetting Seth flew out the window. Getting Seth became her new agenda.

~.~

Seth didn't like this. He didn't like it all. Valentine's Day alone had been bad enough. Seemed like all his high school cronies were married or engaged. Another Sunday dinner at his parents' house without Selena felt a hell of a lot worse than the wedding or Valentine's Day.

"Here, could you hold Sean while I check and see if Amanda's all right?" Connor handed him a bundle of smelly baby. Just what Seth needed. "She's been in the bathroom for at least fifteen minutes."

"Your wife's pregnant with twins, Connor. She probably has lots of girl stuff to do." His brother took off. One of Sean's tiny hands moved, the fingers tickling Seth's face. He froze when the baby smiled up at him, all gums and spit. "Listen little guy, don't get too comfortable. This is temporary, hear me?"

Although his mom's meatloaf was one of Seth's favorites, this Sunday it tasted like sawdust. He had been waiting for a good time to cut out when Connor caught him. Wasn't it enough that Cameron had popped the question this weekend? The family was celebrating Harper's engagement. The fact that Selena happened to be there with Harper turned his stomach. That wouldn't help his case one bit.

With a wet gurgle, Sean worked at cramming both fists into his mouth. Maybe Seth should have stayed home with the cat. From what he could see, cats were easier than kids but maybe just as expensive. He'd spent the whole day buying supplies. Darn kitten followed him wherever he went in the house and hadn't seemed pleased to see him leave.

Sean started to cry. Seth jiggled him. The kid sounded outraged, fists waving while his face turned pink. Seth swayed. Nope, no difference.

"Up on your shoulder," Mark told him across the table. Two kids and Mark was an expert. Younger than Seth by one year, he'd married right out college. In high school, Mark hadn't played sports. Instead he'd lived in the computer lab—a total nerd. Now he created video games, making money hand over fist, as their father liked to say. Dad was proud of Mark.

Seth shifted Sean onto his shoulder. Sometimes he wished he'd gone on to school. Instead, the wail of the ambulance siren had called to him. He loved being an EMT. Loved never knowing what the day would bring. High school had been so boring, except for the sports. How many detentions had he racked up for falling asleep in class?

How long would Amanda be in there? He hoped everything was all right. Most of the time Sean was a pretty cute kid. Seth was looking forward to showing him how to throw a football. If he would just stop crying.

His mother slipped into the chair next to him. "Now what's this I hear about Selena?"

Seth pretended to be very busy with Sean, patting him on the back. "Listen, little dude, what's the problem?" The baby burped. Gross, but the noise stopped.

"Seth? Your mother asked you something." Reenie was wearing her tell-me-or-else look.

"She's visiting Harper."

"Valentine's Day and your girlfriend's off visiting your sister? I want to know why."

Sure. Right. How much had Connor and Amanda spilled when they got home from the wedding? All kinds of excuses formed in his mind. But none of her children could ever put anything over on

Reenie. "We are, uh, working things out."

He heard someone snort in back of him. McKenna was carrying a huge heart-shaped cake to the table. His mother made this cake every year around Valentine's Day. Soon as the kids were old enough, they learned to sprinkle cinnamon hearts on top of the puffy white frosting.

"You know I've always liked Selena," his mother murmured. Thank goodness there was so much commotion that no one else could hear. "She's good for you."

"I know that, Mom." Oh, for God's sake. Like he didn't break into a cold sweat every time he thought of losing Selena forever. Only his mother could make him feel like he was four years old again. When Sean started fussing again, Seth almost felt relieved. Reaching out, his mother scooped the baby from his arms. "Don't disappoint me, Seth."

Ah, the fatal "don't disappoint me." The rest of the table politely looked the other way, talking about the cake, the snow, anything while his mother browbeat him in true Kirkpatrick fashion.

"What do you think of your sister's engagement?"

Seth studied the cake McKenna had just set down. "Cameron's a great guy. They deserve each other."

"Good people aren't easy to find, son. Peggy Dwyer's daughter married that man she met in Vegas? Divorce just came through. We don't want that in this family."

He hated the concern pinching his mother's features. And she wasn't finished. "Soon both my girls will be married."

Only two boys to go. Mothers hold their own kind of score sheet. When Seth tried to speak, his throat felt tight and dry. He reached for his glass of water. "I'm happy for her, Mom. Really. When's the date?"

"No date yet. I hope Harper's not planning on the summer." Picking up a napkin, his mother fanned flushed cheeks.

Thank God Connor returned to the table, Amanda plodding along behind him. Her face glowed and he loved to see them as parents. That's what people did in his family: They married and had babies. Amanda took little Sean and his mother moved on. Seth's breathing had just returned to normal when McKenna slid into the chair his mother had vacated.

"So, how's your weekend going?" His sister pinned him with those greenish-brown eyes.

Chapter 8

"As much fun as a heart attack." Seth would not let McKenna get to him. "Delivered any babies this weekend?"

"Yep. Darling little boy yesterday." She flashed the huge rock Logan had given her at Christmas. Seth's eyes swerved away, like he was avoiding the scene of a crime. He was happy for his sister but her engagement wasn't helping his case with Selena. Before that, he'd been really happy with his relationship.

That thought hit him like a stun gun. Selena made him happy...wildly happy. He'd never put his feelings into those words before. McKenna was looking at him like he'd just fallen off the stupid truck.

He struggled to pull his thoughts together. "You, ah, you guys decided where you're going to have the ceremony?"

"Santa Fe. You coming?"

He jerked back. "Hey, that hurts. I'm in the wedding party, r-remember? We all are, as far as I know."

His sister had something besides the wedding on her mind. Her fingers drummed on the table. Shoving his chair back, Seth grabbed his empty plate and left for the kitchen. McKenna followed right behind him.

"What? Spit it out." Good thing this room was empty. He

added his plate to the stack next to the sink.

"When are you going to tell Selena about the ADD?"

That? "It's none of her business. A man's got to have some privacy."

The noise McKenna made was funny when they were in grade school. Now it was just plain insulting. "If *she's* your business, then she has a right to know."

"But it has n-nothing to d-do with us."

"Seth, how can you say that? After all your sessions with the speech therapists, I can always tell when you're under stress. And right now? You are." By this time she was whispering. Maybe hissing was more like it.

"All in g-good time." Seth pressed his lips together so tight, they hurt.

"You're keeping her out."

"I've got my reasons."

"If pride is one of them, I'm not buying it."

Had he even breathed in the last sixty seconds? "It's my life and it's private."

"Well if you want Selena in your life, it's time to share. Throw her a line, Seth. You have to let her in." Wearing her cocky grin, McKenna glanced at her watch. "Well, got to head out to the airport and pick up Selena."

Really? "No need. I'm on it."

"Really? You'd do that for me?" His sister's lips tilted into a devilish grin.

"You bet." Grabbing his jacket, he dashed out the door. Seth didn't want to give McKenna time to change her mind. O'Hare was a long ride from Oak Park and she should be glad that he was going.

Was he kidding himself? McKenna had her own agenda and tonight he didn't care.

Seth needed that time on the road to figure out what to say. His tongue felt velcroed to the roof of his mouth. He'd forgotten his gloves and the steering wheel was freezing. The brown bomber jacket wasn't the warmest one he had, but it made him look like a cool dude. Tonight he needed all the help he could get. The heat didn't kick in until he reached Hwy 294. Now if he could just get comfortable with what he had to say.

He couldn't mess up tonight. He just could not. Sweat poured off him and he turned the heat off. This felt like last Christmas when he watched the news, scared to death that Connor was the fireman trapped in the five-alarm fire in Berwyn.

What if Selena was furious when she saw him? She might go all-out, hot-Latin-woman ballistic, hands flying and bi-lingual madness slapping him every which way. From the very start, he'd loved Selena's spirit. She lived with passion—a woman you'd want on your side when the going gets tough. McKenna had told him that Selena was dynamite in the delivery room. "She thinks with her hands and her heart." That Guatemalan mission trip? Selena's idea from the start. The natives loved her because they knew she really cared. Her passion drew a team of volunteer professionals city-wide. Who could resist her kind of energy?

But tonight was personal. Above all else, he wanted to avoid getting kicked to the curb. Again. Somehow he had to edge back up onto Selena's main road. Hadn't he always been her "Main Man"?

What if he was still history? What if Harper's engagement made her bat-shit crazy? Talk about bad timing. Selena hadn't answered one of his texts. Was she meeting other guys in Savannah? Cameron probably had a boatload of friends. His mother's meatloaf turned over in his stomach.

A trucker cut him off and Seth laid on his horn. The air turned blue with his language. Then it hit him. He was mad at himself, not the guy who hadn't used his side view mirror. Mad and terrified. The last couple weeks had been hell.

What could he say tonight that would turn up the heat in Selena's flashing brown eyes? Words were not his strong suit.

"Look, I know you're surprised to see me. I just thought I'd help McKenna out."

Nope. That would get him nowhere and rightly so.

"Baby, I missed you so much. I was hoping we could talk."

Better. Now he had something with feeling. Maybe he could channel Connor or Malcolm. They were both great with words.

"Selena, you've got this all wrong. And I am totally clueless."

Clueless? He could almost hear his dad laughing. Where would they go from there?

Checking both side view mirrors, he changed lanes.

"Never let a woman know you've screwed up." That had been rule number one from Big Mike when the boys were growing up. Chief of the Fire Department, his dad always knew what he was doing. If he didn't? Well, Mom and the kids never found out. Big Mike moved forward like a tank. One time he used brown shoe polish on Joe's gray shoes. That's when they discovered their father was color blind. "I always thought something was a little off," he'd laughed.

But he never admitted he was wrong. Seth didn't want to be like that. He also didn't want to make a fool out of himself.

Traffic slowed to a crawl and his hands hurt from mauling the steering wheel. What if he was late? Didn't matter what time it was, traffic on 294 was always bumper-crunching time. Seth hated all the lanes, too hard to think and plan. He edged along, jerking into any opening, any line of traffic inching forward.

Would logic work with her?

Probably not. But how could she possibly think he'd been going out on her? He was dreaming, for Pete's sake, when he mentioned Sissy. Sure, some women thought he was the bomb, and his brothers called him a stud muffin, but he'd left that all behind. For her.

Yes, he still had his man cave in the basement but he'd been meaning to clear out all those pictures for a long time. He'd changed a lot for Selena and he'd made those changes because he wanted to. The truth was, now he needed words, the right words to persuade her that she was special to him. The only one.

"Selena, you are now my one and only."

Sounded lame and he knew it.

Language wasn't his strength. He couldn't even make it through the first quarter of French in high school. Behind him a horn blared and Seth stepped on the gas. The car shot forward and he had to slam on the brakes to avoid rear-ending a Toyota.

"Who flunks English?" His mother had demanded sophomore year. "You speak English, right?" Why hadn't he studied vocabulary more, maybe taken that public speaking class he'd blown off?

But there was another issue. The one he never talked about. And this was not the time.

Time was running out. His mother's egg timer? He could almost feel that salt pouring down his throat. Pretty soon he'd be at the turnoff for the airport. Almost there and no idea what to say. Had to be from his heart, which was a long way from the part of him clamoring for attention.

He was suffering from severe Selena deprivation.

But it wasn't just the sex. The realization lifted his foot from the pedal.

No. For once, that wasn't it. Not that sex with Selena wasn't off the charts. It was. But he missed more than just that. Her throaty chuckle. Her dark, soft curls. The velvety brown eyes that always seemed to understand him better than he understood himself. The way she finished his sentences, mainly because he didn't have the words.

He'd never remember all this stuff. All the things he had to say.

He'd never remember the words.

Following the signs to the parking area, he wished he had written it all down. He needed more time.

~~

The plane landed with a slight bump. Selena had dozed most of the way back from Savannah, head crammed against the cold window. Now her neck ached and her mouth felt dry and papery. All around her, passengers were grabbing their carry-ons, trying to stand up in the cramped quarters. She was still thinking about the visit to Savannah and the talks with Harper. Sure, they'd had fun shopping, but the conversations helped her understand Seth and men a little better.

Savannah had been a fun getaway but Cameron's proposal had left her with a bittersweet taste. Why hadn't she seen this coming? Proposing on Valentine's Day made sense. The timing was right. But for her, witnessing a proposal was right up there with inhaling fertilizer. Toxic stuff.

The looks on the couple's faces said it all. They belonged together. But most of all, Cameron cherished Harper. It made Selena's nose stuffy, remembering the way he held her after he slipped the ring on her finger. Sniffling, Selena stood up, grabbed her bag from the overhead compartment and followed the line moving slowly toward the exit.

Bella had been beside herself with happiness. "I always wanted to call you Mom."

"Fine with me," Harper said. "You can call me Mom now."

"Mom." Bella's lips formed a wide O before closing with a kiss on Harper's cheek. Had there been a dry eye in the place? Even the waitress was hauling out a tissue. Tears brimmed in the eyes of Cameron's mother and sister. Unlike Seth's mom and the whole bunch, Cameron's family didn't seem to show affection openly.

Probably not a hugging group, from what she'd seen. But they seemed to like Harper. Who could help but love Harper Kirkpatrick?"

The rightness of it all made Selena sad. In so many ways, Cameron reminded her of Seth—polite, kind and considerate, but with a streak of bad boy in him. Her stomach tightened with longing.

She'd run this all past McKenna when she saw her in a few seconds.

Almost to the exit door, Selena felt the shift in temperature. She'd be glad to get out of the recirculated air that everyone knew was unhealthy. Head down, she pulled her luggage up the carpeted ramp and then made tracks down the corridor. Because she didn't want to crush her boots in the small case, she'd decided to wear them and they clicked on the tile floor.

No doubt McKenna would be excited about her little sister's engagement. Lots of chitchat in the car going home. When she reached the gate, Selena pasted a smile on her face and lifted her chin.

And there he was. She stumbled in her new boots. Tall, broad-shouldered and heart-breakingly handsome, Seth gave her a smile that didn't look so confident. *Ah, pobrecito.* His eyes searched her face like he was trying to read his GPS. The auburn hair was pushed back and the collar of his bomber jacket pulled up. Her resolve melted under a heated surge of longing.

Nothing beat coming home to the man she loved.

That feeling must've shown on her face because Seth opened

his arms. Exactly where she wanted to be. Darn it all, she stepped right into them. The kiss should've made her blush. She pressed her entire body into his, loving how every curve found a snug resting place. Heck, she was a starving woman and Seth Kirkpatrick was her private banquet. At least, she liked to think that.

"Babe, I've missed you," he whispered, pulling her out of the foot traffic. "Let's get out of here."

Whole body trembling, she could only nod.

Seth snagged her bag and they streaked toward the exit. Being with him felt so good—just like old times. When they reached the parking garage, he backed her up against the cinderblock, did a full body block and kissed her until her head spun. "There are cameras all over this place," she finally whispered on a ragged breath.

"Probably glad to have something worthwhile to watch." Cupping her chin in his hands like she just might break, he gazed at her. His eyes caressed her like a summer breeze and she trembled. One more kiss kicked her into full out shudder. Seth groaned. "Come on."

When they reached his car, he heaved her bag into the back and then they were off. All the way back to his place, their hands were busy. No words, just strokes, caresses that had always been their own language. He rested one hand on her thigh and she played with the back of his hair. His hand crept higher. Her fingers tugged tightly.

These were their words. Always had been.

She could read each stroke like braille.

When a small voice in her head urged caution, she shut it down fast. Tonight she knew what she needed. Amazing that the snow didn't melt into steamy rivulets under their feet as they stumbled up the steps from his garage and into the kitchen. Seth slammed the door shut behind them and clothes went flying. First the coats, then the sweaters. They ripped them off. Let them lie. No need to pick them up. No time to straighten anything.

She just. Needed. Him.

His kisses that left her gasping.

Caresses that left her wanting more.

Heat that ravaged her body.

As they staggered up the stairs, his hands ran over the new boots she'd forgotten to kick off. "Nice."

"I just bought them." Almost added *for you*, but the words clotted in her throat.

"We might keep those on."

"They've been outside."

"So have I."

They reached his room, where his eyes did a thorough sweep of her body before she tugged him onto the bed.

Seth got to work. "Maybe we'll take the boots off." When he ran his hands over the leather before he unzipped, she knew she'd chosen well. Harper would be pleased. One boot hit the floor and then the other. Coiling up to meet him, she trailed her lips over his bare chest. His pecs flexed and he moaned. "Selena."

"Oh, Seth, I've missed you so much."

His eyes flew open as if he'd just remembered something.

"What is it?" Her galloping heart should be shaking the bed.

He sucked in a breath. The pulse at the base of his neck picked up speed. "I've done so much for you...I mean, *you've* done—"

"Not now, Seth. *Por favor.*"

His lips still moved. "Right now, you're my..."

She didn't want to hear it. Tonight she just wanted to feel. With deep coaxing kisses, she brought him back into the moment. Seth was the only man she ever wanted to love. Words weren't necessary. She kept telling her heart that, while her mind whispered something different. How she wished she had mental earplugs.

Their bodies knew the way. She flicked open the button of his jeans, the zipper rasped and he kicked them away. No time for words. No time for thinking.

Thank God he was in a hurry.

So intense, so familiar, so satisfying when they moved together that tears trailed down her cheeks.

Seth stopped. "Selena, what's wrong?"

"Nothing. Don't stop. Please." Pulling him close so he couldn't see her cry, she got back into it. Last thing she wanted was for him to see how badly she'd missed him. She'd thought she'd never make love to him again. Her life had stretched bleak in front of her, like a field that needed planting.

A future without his loving. Would he give her loving but not his love? Was that even possible?

Selena slammed the trapdoor of her mind. She told herself this night was for her but her thoughts circled back, persistent and irritating.

What had he said? He'd done so much for her? What was that

about?

Don't overthink it.

Seth took her with tenderness that just about broke her heart. After all, the man knew all her hot spots. And he knew how to stoke that heat. Oh, so slowly, he took her and loved her. That's what he was doing. He was loving her with his body. Were words so necessary? Arching her back, Selena felt the train screaming toward her. She wanted to lie down on the tracks and feel it whoosh over her.

Feel the relief. Treasure the afterglow.

They struck their own rhythm, knew the way so well, got to the station just in time.

Afterwards, legs tangled in the sheets, she lay back and whispered. "Ah, *mi amor*, I love you so." The words slipped out, so natural and right.

But maybe not.

The room turned quiet. She felt his intake of breath and wanted to cut out her tongue.

Selena told herself she didn't need the words from him. But her heart clamored for them. Her body felt satisfied but her heart coiled up at the foot of the bed like a snake and hissed, *Now what, Selena?*

In her arms, Seth began to sweat big time.

"S-selena, you are now my... I mean, I...." Ducking his head, Seth nuzzled her cheek. Like he didn't want to look at her.

Her heart slowed, turned hard and hurtful, like a shoreline pebble in her sandal. She was trying to figure out how to get out of here when something furry shot out of nowhere and landed on her bare chest.

She screamed. Rats? A bat? "Seth. *Qué es esto?* What the... ?" The animal sprang onto the nightstand, blue eyes glowing in the dark.

"Hey, don't scare him. Come 'ere, Shadow." Plucking a kitten from the side table, Seth settled it against his chest. Selena's fear subsided. The purring rippled through the room like rich corduroy.

"When did you get a cat?" She pulled the sheet up.

Petting the furry bundle, Seth grinned sheepishly. "I didn't. He found me. Here, pet him."

She reached out, just to have something to do with her hands. Anything to get Seth's mind off the words that lay abandoned between them. The kitten looked up at her and arched when Selena smoothed a hand down its back. "Sure is a cute little thing." Every farm her family ever worked for had wild cats to keep down the field mice. She gave Seth's new kitten a careful look. "This is a girl, Seth. *Una muchacha.*"

"No kidding?" Settling back, Seth tucked his arms behind his head. "That's okay, Shadow, I still love you. Good thing I didn't name him Jake or Jerry, right?"

Their laughter healed one hurt and ripped open another.

Sure, he could tell the cat he loved her.

She handed Shadow back. "Well, big trip. Guess I'm tired."

Rolling onto her side, she pretended to fall asleep. The kitten settled between them. Only when Seth's breathing evened out did she let out an exasperated sigh.

Okay, she'd tried plan A. Now for plan B. Did she have one?

Chapter 9

The cold hardwood floor curled Selena's toes when she slid out of bed early the next morning. Pitch dark and Seth was sound asleep on his tummy. Shadow snoozed, plastered against his legs. She wanted to smooth his bad boy hair, run a hand over his broad shoulders. But she didn't. She'd just be making a bad situation worse.

Man, it was cold and her teeth chattered. Snatching her clothes from the floor, she scooped up her boots and crept toward the door. Shadow's eyes followed her in the dark, two glowing pinpoints, but the cat decided to stay with Seth. Selena didn't blame her. Regret twisted in her gut as she slipped from the room. Traitorous parts of her body were doing a memorial happy dance. She loved Seth and last night had been everything she'd dreamed about in Savannah. Except for the end.

He hadn't said the words. In fact, *she'd* been the one who spoke up in a weak moment. *I love you.* How had that slipped out?

Time to face the facts.

Seth wasn't ready for commitment. He might never be ready.

Standing in the cold hallway with Seth's grandfather clock ticking, she had one leg in her jeans when it hit her. She hadn't driven. *Idiota.* She'd rather stick a pin in her eyes than wake Seth up.

Who lived in this area? Bethany, the other midwife in their practice. *Thank you, God.*

Fully dressed with boots in hand, she crept down the stairs and back toward the kitchen. Seth had kept the old pantry when he did his renovations. Stepping inside, she pulled out her phone and scrolled to favorites. "Hey, have you left for work yet?" she whispered when Bethany picked up.

"No, and why are you whispering?"

"Because I don't want to wake Seth up."

"Thought you broke up with him."

Sigh. "I fell off the wagon last night."

Silence. Then, "Right. Got it."

But how could Bethany understand? She was engaged to Walt, her high school sweetheart. From what Selena could see, they'd been committed to each other since sophomore year. Not exciting, but Selena wasn't looking for that craziness anymore.

"I don't have my car. Can you pick me up at Cozy Corner? I'll watch for you."

"Sure. Be there in half an hour."

"Thanks, Bethany. I owe you."

Pocketing her phone, Selena tiptoed back to the front door, grabbed her coat from the floor and pulled it on. The cold, dry air outside took her breath away. Snow squeaked under her boots when she began to walk. She sure wasn't in Savannah anymore.

The Cozy Corner was five blocks away and Selena broke into a jog to warm up. The walks weren't all shoveled so she had to be careful. It wasn't until she hit Harlem Avenue that Selena realized she'd left her suitcase at Seth's house. Perfect. All her makeup and some of her clothes were in the small carry-on. Thank goodness the phone had been in her jean pocket or she'd really be in trouble.

Last night hit her like a runaway freight train. Skidding to a halt on the hard-packed snow, she folded over, hands on her knees. A police car cruised by and the window rolled down. "Everything okay?" the officer called out.

She straightened. "Fine. Everything's just fine. Have a great day." Thank goodness he didn't look familiar. Because Seth's father was a retired fireman, policemen often showed up at the family gatherings. The two groups worked closely. This morning she sure as heck didn't want to be recognized.

Ears stinging, she broke into a quick walk. On her way to the Cozy Corner, she dashed into an all-night drug store for mascara, lipstick and eyeliner. By the time she reached the coffee shop, the dark sky had paled to gray.

No matter what time it was, Cozy Corner always had customers. Cream and sugar in her coffee and Selena was back in business. "And I'll have the Belgian waffle and two eggs over easy." The order came out naturally, what she always got. Taking her mug into the restroom she worked on her makeup. Not much she could do for the bloodshot eyes though. Well, she could stop crying. Right, and that would be like trying to jam on the top of a pressure cooker in full steam.

Dashing some lipstick on the tips of her fingers, she rubbed them on her cheeks for some color and stood back. Not great but it would have to do. Touring back through the coffee shop, she slid the mug onto the counter and sat down. But she didn't feel hungry. Her eggs cooled while Selena pushed them around on the heavy crockery plate. She even picked at the Belgian waffle. How well she remembered feeding one to Seth last fall. He'd laughed, sticky syrup all over his lips when he kissed her. When Bethany pulled up outside in her sensible beige sedan, she threw some bills on the counter and dashed outside.

"Thanks a bunch," she told her colleague, climbing into the warm car and rubbing her hands under a warm jet of air.

"Not a problem." Pulling away from the curb, Bethany shot her a concerned look. "You okay?"

"As good as a girl can feel who's fallen off the wagon."

"I'm so sorry, Selena. I didn't realize, you know, that you were an alcoholic."

"Not that kind of wagon, Bethany. You know." She hitched a shoulder.

Only Bethany probably didn't. The newest addition to their team was as sensible and sweet as her dimples. Probably a homecoming queen, the type of girl Selena could never be. You don't come from the picking fields and be voted a high school sweetheart. She never stayed in one school long enough. Selena had scratched her way through high school and college, living in a ton of places, piecing her education together. Back then, she had no idea what an extra curricular activity was. Corn detassling?

The Eisenhower Expressway had been ploughed but the falling snow churned under the tires and kept traffic to a crawl. "Can we turn on some music?" Jumpy, Selena reached for the buttons.

"I'm driving, Selena. Have to concentrate."

"Oh, right." Yep, Bethany was sensible. Probably a girl who could draw a line with a man and then stay on her side. Their headlights swept the falling snow on the road and Savannah felt more distant than Mars. Memories of the proposal dinner with Cameron and Harper battled with thoughts of last night. Anger dried her tears, but the only person she was mad at was herself.

Qué lástima, chica. Didn't she know better?

You can't change people. Her mother taught her that when she'd complain about a farmer who'd been rude. "Do your best and smile, cariña," her mother would tell her. "And keep your head up. Always." Although she'd thought she could accept Seth for what he was, what they had, her time with Harper and Cameron had taught her differently. Last night had been wonderful but this morning her heart felt empty.

She'd said the L word but he hadn't.

Soon they passed under the gigantic post office that loomed over the entry to downtown Chicago. Thank goodness Bethany knew the back streets to avoid the crush of Michigan Avenue. Before too long, they were pulling into the parking garage at the hospital. All the midwives parked on the top level, where the view was spectacular.

"Thanks so much, Bethany." Selena avoided her friend's eyes when they got out of the car and walked to the elevators. How could a girl like Bethany ever imagine the madness that had possessed Selena last night?

Bethany's hug surprised her. "Any time, Selena. I'm so sorry."

They walked the rest of the way in silence.

Dorothy was busy getting the office up and running when they passed through the reception area. While Bethany continued to her office, McKenna waylaid Selena and tugged her from the hall.

"How was your trip? Was Harper totally surprised by the ring?"

"Sure looked like it." The joy on Harper's face would stay with Selena a long time. "They're such a great couple."

"Okay, we know that. Maybe I should ask how *you're* feeling about Harper's engagement?" McKenna had a way of drilling down fast.

"I'm happy for her. They're crazy about each other. Bella was thrilled. She must have called Harper Mom ten times before we left that restaurant. And I got to meet Cameron's mother and his sister. All good."

Facts, just the facts. So much easier to talk about another woman's relationship. Selena felt her smile go south.

McKenna's eyes narrowed. "Hey, sure you're okay?"

"Not really. I left all my clothes and makeup at your brother's house last night."

"You can get all that later, right? Or Seth can drop it off here?" Hope and curiosity glimmered in McKenna's eyes.

"Not going to happen." She had to help McKenna understand this without making her feel guilty for sending Seth to O'Hare. "Last night was a mistake. I'm not proud of it."

McKenna groaned. "Oh, no. I was hoping you two would have time to talk."

"I fell off the wagon and enjoyed it. Have to be honest. But it didn't change anything. *Stúpida!*" She pushed away from the doorway. "McKenna, I've got to move on."

Lips tight, McKenna didn't say another word and Selena left.

All day she stoked her self-disgust, grateful for the full schedule.

Just when things eased up, Lucy Mandel and her husband Rob checked in to have their twins. Since these were their first children, the process took a while. Grateful, Selena fell into the process of labor and delivery. No wandering thoughts here. Those red squalling infants were a prize worth waiting for. If anything, they strengthened Selena's resolve. Seeing the joy on Lucy's face, Selena knew she wanted that for herself and time was a wasting. The sky was pitch black when Selena changed in the locker room. This time, she was not going to try to catch a ride. Instead, she called a cab.

As the cabbie tore down the Dan Ryan toward Wrigleyville, Selena checked her messages but didn't open the ones from Seth. Instead she sent her own. "Please give my suitcase to McKenna the next time you see her."

Maybe this was the chicken's way out, but a conversation? She couldn't handle it right now.

~.~

When Seth woke up that Monday morning, the bed felt empty. He ran one hand over the cool sheet next to him and pushed up on his elbows. Damn. "Selena?"

Her name echoed in the cold room. Stretching, Shadow looked at him and meowed. "Yeah, I know you're hungry. But where'd she go?"

Slumping back onto the pillow he raked his fingers through his hair. He had a chance to make it right and he'd blown it. What had he done? Or was it something he said? He'd thought she'd come back to him. That things were all right. They sure felt all right but now, he didn't know.

All that practicing in the car hadn't helped a bit. What had he mumbled? I've done a lot for you instead of you've done a lot for me? With a groan that sent Shadow flying off the bed, he fell back and threw on arm over his eyes. Selena told him she loved him and he couldn't find the words. He wanted the words to be perfect. To say what he meant. Embarrassment singed his cheeks. Damn, of course he loved her. Had almost died while she was away.

He loved her. Could it be that simple? He let the words sink in.

Tossing back the sheet, he sprang out of bed and jammed his toe against Selena's suitcase. Right foot throbbing, he scooped up a handful of clothes from the open bag and buried his face in it. Breathing in her scent, he felt the intense reaction that had started the first time he saw her at the Purple Frog.

Selena had been sitting in a booth with McKenna. Throwing back her long dark curls, she was laughing, dark eyes flashing and delicate hands fluttering. Chicago had a lot of women but this girl was different. Earthy but feminine. Glancing up, she caught him staring and smiled. He stopped breathing.

Those eyes. Her full lips. Not a girl who put on airs, just direct and bold. Her dark eyes challenged him and he tripped over his own feet to get to her. From what he could see, at least three other guys had this woman on their radar. But she was looking straight at him and sitting with *his* sister. Seth made his move.

"Hey, how'd you get here?"

"A car?" She grinned up at him, all saucy and sexy.

The whole table cracked up and he'd felt his face flush.

"No I mean, w-where did you come from? Friend of my sister?"

Take it slow, his mother had always told him. Take it slow so you don't stumble over your words.

"This is my subtle brother Seth." McKenna had introduced them. Selena's long lashes feathered over her blushing cheeks. Then she made direct eye contact and moved over. Their mutual attraction had been just that strong. It didn't take long for the others to disappear. They'd spent three hours talking, although it felt more like ten minutes.

They'd never looked back.

So why couldn't he look forward?

Going to the head of the stairs, he leaned over the railing and called again. "Babe? Selena? You here?"

Only silence. Silence and a forgotten bag.

Like she'd left in a hurry. Like she'd had second thoughts.

"Damn." With Shadow winding herself around his legs, he stumbled into the bathroom for a shower. He got the water as hot as he could stand it and then flipped on the cold water.

He'd blown it. The night had felt so darn good, but obviously not to her.

The words. This had to do with the words.

He wasn't on until second shift so he stopped at his parents' house. His father had called him about fixing a garage door that had come off the trolley so he went over. Big mistake. His mother grabbed him first, jabbering about Harper's engagement. But he didn't say much.

After pouring him a mug of coffee, she shoved it at him. "Get out of bed on the wrong side this morning, Seth?"

He took the mug from her hand. "I don't see what all the fuss is about." The coffee had no taste.

"Don't you want to see your sisters happy? Don't you want to see them settled in their lives with good partners?"

Swirling the coffee in his mug, he couldn't meet his mother's eyes. His dad appeared in the door. "Okay, could we get on with the garage door?"

Seth set the mug down so fast, the coffee slopped over the edge. His mother grabbed a towel. He could feel her eyes drilling a hole in his back as he followed his father out the door. The cold air cleared his head on the way to the detached garage. Struggling with the tension in the trolley was no joke, but Seth wanted a challenge today. He wanted to work with his hands because he knew he could do that. They both had to be really careful or the wire might snap back at them. But after a few minutes they had it.

"Everything all right, son?" Washing his hands at the garage sink, his father studied him.

"Sure. Of course." In the Kirkpatrick family, the boys didn't have heart-to-heart talks with their dad. Big Mike doled out advice with a liberal spoon. But as far as Seth knew, Malcolm was about the only son who really opened up with their father. Connor and

Seth, and Mark and Joe kept things to themselves. Soon after that, Seth left.

His mood worsened as the day wore on with no word from Selena. A heart patient, two accidents on the ice and then the type of injury he really hated. Domestic dispute. When he showed up at the apartment, the young woman on the kitchen floor had not run into a cupboard. That was pretty clear. She was bleeding from the head, her arm at an odd angle, and she was crying. The cop took notes while Seth and Sissy stopped the bleeding and got the gurney ready.

"Must have left that cupboard open last night," the young woman mumbled, disoriented and frightened. He suspected a broken jaw, the way she was talking.

"Yeah, right." Seth exchanged a glance with the cop. How often did they hear this?

Of course, he had to be working with Sissy Hanson. Life wasn't bad enough today. He'd been giving her a wide berth.

Despite her insistence about the cupboard, the woman agreed to go to the hospital. She couldn't walk and was having trouble speaking. The nurses in the ER took over from there.

"So, do we get a lot of these?" Sissy asked him on the way back to the EMS Limited offices.

"Get used to it."

Usually all smiles, Sissy wasn't taking this well. She was young and from what he could see she was just testing out the EMT role. Wanted to see if it was a good fit. Her little girl giggles might be a big turn on for some guys. Not him. Now Selena? She would've been reading that girl in the apartment the riot act, telling her to move out. Sissy looked horrified. He gave her three months on this job before she bailed.

The next call was in a northern area of Oak Park. Sirens wailing, they tore up Harlem Avenue. Dispatch said a neighbor had found an older woman unresponsive. Like a lot of the buildings in this area, the redbrick apartment had probably been built in the 1940s. Grabbing their bags, Seth and Sissy dashed inside and raced up to the third floor. A young woman who said she was their neighbor was trying to give CPR to an older woman stretched out on the living room floor. Her husband hovered above the two, looking like he might pass out himself. The young woman glanced up. "Henry called me. I took this class…"

"I'll take over from here, ma'am."

The victim's face was ashen and she was about his mother's age. Seth got to work with chest compressions and rescue breaths, trying to ignore the fact that this patient could have been his mother. When he paused and checked for vitals, he detected a faint heartbeat. In the background, he heard Sissy comforting the husband. "Now, see, everything will be just fine."

Not exactly what a tech should tell a family member and he'd have to talk to her. "Let's get her to the hospital."

Sissy helped him move the woman onto the gurney and they were out the door, taking it easy on the narrow stairs. The neighbor would follow with the husband.

While they were lifting the gurney into the back of the ambulance, the husband came close and squeezed his wife's hand.

"Vicky, honey. You're going to be all right, okay?" Her eyelids fluttered open and she tried to smile.

Seth had been at this for a while. Still, this guy got to him.

"We gotta get going, Seth, right?" Sissy whispered.

"Just give him a second."

The wife squeezed her husband's hand. "I'll be fine, Harry. Fine."

"You better be." Watching the old guy fight back tears was painful. "You know, we got bingo Friday night."

Nodding, the lady squeezed her eyes shut.

"Okay, let's hit the road, sir. Gotta get your wife to the hospital. You drive, Sissy."

Seth hopped in next to the woman and Sissy climbed behind the wheel. As he worked with his patient, Seth wondered who would comfort him if anything ever happened. Only his family? For the first time ever, his family didn't feel like enough.

The case seemed to be working like clockwork when the woman coded. Not that unusual and he grabbed the paddles. Once. And again. And again. Nothing worked. Nausea roiled in his stomach and panic screamed across his chest.

Nothing worked. Had he been too busy with his own stuff?

"Heart probably just not that strong," the nurse told him later as he stood there in the ER, watching them take the husband back. "Sometimes there's nothing you can do."

That night after he punched out, he drove down to Selena's neighborhood near Wrigley Field. Even though getting to her place often took an hour from Oak Park, he'd never asked her to move in with him. They'd swapped keys but avoided that next step. Had it been her or him? The windows of her second floor apartment were dark. Using his key, he let himself into the foyer and climbed to the second floor. The tiled hallway smelled of pizza and dry radiator air. He propped her suitcase against the door.

For a second Seth stood there, tapping the key against his palm. She could be awake, reading in bed. But after that last run, he felt unsteady. What could he say that could fix this?

Nothing. Nothing he ever said was right.

Feeling like he had a forty-pound pack on his shoulders, Seth left. No use making this worse. In the old days, she would have welcomed him inside. He'd tell her about today because she knew just how this felt.

If he could talk to her about someone else's problems, why couldn't he tell her about his childhood? He had to try.

Chapter 10

Selena sat in the Purple Frog, listening to Whitney Houston belt out a song about loving somebody forever. She knew the feeling. Could have written the song. Since her return from Savannah, she'd been avoiding Seth. She didn't answer his calls and tried not to read his texts.

Tried but wasn't always successful.

Heck, she knew some of them by heart.

Why did you leave so early?

And later...*You mad or something?*

Then much later...*How can I make this right?*

The waiter brought a basket of peanuts. "Friend's coming," she told him. After all her time with Seth, it felt strange to be waiting for another man. Thank God that cute waiter wasn't around. She couldn't be responsible for her actions tonight.

The peanuts felt salty and gritty in her fingers. She crushed the shells one by one and popped the peanuts into her mouth. They felt like marbles. How could peanuts not have any flavor? Still, she went through the motions. Chewing and swallowing gave her something to do.

As usual, the Purple Frog was crowded and she saw a few people she knew. Only two blocks from the hospital, the place was a hangout with good food and background music everyone recognized. Gary Rice was easy to spot when he came through the door. Selena stood up and waved.

Heads turned when the young obstetrician eased through crowd. A few of the nurses waylaid him, eyes clinging when he continued to Selena's booth. By tomorrow, the hospital hotline would have the two of them married. Lean and loose limbed, Gary was a runner. A couple times she'd joined him on an early morning run and they paced themselves along the paths that skirted the lake. The running kept him human, Gary always joked. The guy was easy to work with. Women loved him because he was a good listener. If any of their natural childbirth patients had a problem and a caesarean was needed, the midwives called one of the OB/GYNs from Logan's practice. Gary often took the call.

Shedding his leather jacket, Gary slid into the booth across from her and ran a hand through his chestnut curls. Just like McKenna always said, the man was eye candy. "Cold out there. Spring coming soon?"

"Just a rumor."

He grinned. Now that the word was out that she'd broken up with Seth, men looked at her differently. Or was that her imagination? Before, the guys at work had been polite but distant. Now interest sparked in their eyes. They stopped her in the halls, hunched closer and talked longer. One radiology tech had even dropped off coffee last week.

What did it matter? She felt like a jukebox that played one tune. Seth Kirkpatrick.

"You look terrific in purple," Gary told her, signaling to the waiter. "Maybe OB should change the color of its uniforms."

"The catalogues call the color lilac but it's purple to me." She fingered the V-neck. This cozy, fuzzy number might be Seth's favorite but no way was she tucking it away in a drawer. The waiter arrived and they ordered a pitcher of beer and some burgers. At least Whitney Houston had given way to something upbeat by the Avett Brothers.

Gary and Selena traded work stories and she felt the knot at the back of her neck loosen as they talked. At least Gary knew Seth and their history so she didn't have to fill in the blanks.

"Make any progress with the new OB unit?" she asked.

"Yeah, it's coming along. How about you? What are your thoughts about the new unit?" Why had she never noticed Gary's sparkly blue eyes? Maybe because she was so wrapped up in Seth's brown eyes. For the past two years she'd worn blinders.

"Well if it were me, I wouldn't want to be pushed through the halls after just having a baby. I can't wait for the new unit where a woman can labor and deliver in one room." Then her throat closed. Today a husband and family felt out of reach.

The beer and burgers arrived and Gary filled their frosty mugs. That delectable grilled scent awakened her appetite. She'd been surprised when Gary stopped by the office late yesterday and asked if she wanted to hang out at the Purple Frog tonight. She figured why not. Gary was an unthreatening choice. Besides that, he was terminally cute.

"So you and Seth—that's over?"

"That would be a yes." Selena could feel her cheeks flush, like she'd just told a major lie. She took a deep gulp of cold beer, choked and sputtered. Gary handed her napkin. Blotting her eyes, she pushed on. "And you're not dating Mindy anymore? That surprised me."

"You have a dimple." Gary shifted on the vinyl bench seat. "Never noticed it."

She fingered her right cheek. "Right. So, you're ignoring my question?"

His face flushed. "Yeah, Mindy and I are history."

"Want to talk about it?" But she knew the answer. What guy wanted to talk about his feelings?

"Guess we just weren't meant for the long haul. At least not for each other." A shadow passed over Gary's handsome features, like clouds darkening Lake Michigan.

"It happens, right? At first two people connect but over time, they find out they can't go the distance together?" Her voice slowed. Maybe she'd never understand why.

Crunching some peanuts in his hand, Gary tossed them into his mouth one by one. "I think so. I mean, I've been dating for a while and probably so have you. But when it comes to, you know, the one you want forever, I kind of fall back on what I know, which would be my parents. I want what they had."

Thinking back, Selena wanted so much more. "What would that be?"

"Doing stuff together. Liking a lot of the same things so there's no grumbling. At least, that's what I saw growing up. On Sunday mornings they'd do the crossword puzzle together in the newspaper." His lips tipped into a smile, like these were pleasant memories. "From the trips they took to the long walks after dinner—they liked a lot of the same stuff. They felt education was really important so they started college funds for all three of us. Wasn't easy. We hardly ever ate out and rented movies instead of going to the theater. How about you?"

Did having a cold ham sandwich at the edge of the cherry grove count as eating out? Lifting her hamburger bun, she poured more ketchup on her caramelized onions and blue cheese, trying to collect her thoughts. Their backgrounds were so different. "My parents always had common goals, especially when it came to us."

"How many kids in your family, Selena?"

"Five. Three of us went on for higher degrees. I chose healthcare." She was good at skimming over the details.

"Is that why you became involved with Midwives in Action and the summer mission trip to Guatemala?"

Ah, she loved talking about the program she'd started. "Right, I've been given opportunities those women will never have. Time to spread the wealth around."

Enough about her. She took a big bite of her burger. The blue cheese and onions tasted rich on her tongue. Over the past few days, her diet had gone out the window. For some reason, her appetite had come back tonight. After swirling a sweet potato fry in the ketchup, she started to nibble. When she looked up, Gary was staring at her, chewing with a dollop of mustard at one corner of his mouth. Reaching out, she captured the mustard with one fingertip and he blushed.

"Maybe that's why my parents never took us out in public." He ran one hand over his chin with a wry smile. "How did you end up in Chicago?"

"Wanted to see what the big city was like." Her skin still prickled when she remembered how excited she'd been the first time she glimpsed downtown Chicago from the Skyway. "All the tall buildings."

For a few seconds they ate quietly. With Seth, the silences had always felt comfortable. But with Gary? She'd have to get used to this. Her only consolation was that this must feel strange to Gary too. "How does it feel to be sitting here with someone else besides Mindy? Strange?"

"Yep, you bet."

"So when you date someone, what are you looking for?"

"You sound like one of those online dating questionnaires."

"Sorry." So he'd been on those sites? "Just like to get all the cards on the table. Can we think of this as a dry run? In case I do go online?"

"Sure. Why not? Haven't tried one yet but you never know. Let's pretend this is a first meeting. Take your best shot."

Hmm, why not? Selena pushed her plate away. "How would it be if I asked guys something like 'Are you looking for a wine tasting or one fine bottle of wine?'"

Throwing back his head, Gary roared. A couple in the next booth glanced over. "Good God, Selena, that'll make any man think twice. I've always admired your candor. This is just a beer and a burger, okay? Not a marriage proposal."

Her cheeks blazed. "I didn't mean…"

Waving away her concern, Gary nodded. "I know what you mean. I guess we all want that fine bottle of wine. I mean, I'm thirty-two and you're…?"

"Twenty-seven."

"Clock's ticking?"

"Is that right?" When did this turn into a therapy session? She reached for another fry, remembered her thighs and stopped. Summer and bathing suits were right around the corner.

Summer. Summer and McKenna's wedding. Maybe Harper's too. Her stomach spiraled into her boots.

"Don't sell yourself short, Selena."

"What are you talking about?"

"Just saying that Seth doesn't know a good thing when he sees it."

"Maybe." She suspected it was a lot more complicated than that. "Sounds like you've had more dating experience. How do you get over someone?"

Linking his hands behind his head, Gary slouched back. "If I tell you all my secrets, I may have to kill you."

"Somehow I doubt that."

He studied the beams overhead. "Picture him at his worst moment. The time he got to your place one hour late."

"Seth was always on time."

"Didn't he ever wear clothes you hated?"

"I like the way he dressed." In fact, she loved those henley shirts pushed up on the corded muscles of his arms. Her fingertips had total recall and she shivered.

"The time he forgot to shave?"

The brush of his whiskers? Gary's grin said he noticed her dazed smile.

She was being a dimwit. "My turn. How about the time Mindy forgot to shave her legs."

A reminiscent smile softened his lips. "Oh, but I like to shave a woman's legs."

Her stomach clenched. She knew about that firsthand and the sensation had been mind blowing. Seth could be pretty creative. She tried to shake the memory but her legs tingled. "Or when her roots were growing out?" Didn't blondes have that problem? Selena was grateful for her dark hair.

"Everyone's human." Gary grabbed a toothpick from the dispenser. "I don't want to date a perfectionist."

Selena thought back. "How about the time you walked into a bar and every guy in the place said hello to her."

Gary's eyes lightened. "Ah, now you are talking about Seth. The ladies love him. But nothing ever comes of it. You know that, right?"

"I guess." She sighed.

"Really, Selena. Hate to go to bat for another guy, but Seth never fooled around on you."

The lump in her throat felt as big as Wrigley Field.

Balling up his napkin, Gary tossed it to the side. "Here's the thing. I'm not ready for anything or anyone right now. Work is busy and I, well, I want to think about things."

Where was this conversation heading? She turned wary.

"At the hospital, I'm fresh meat." Gary's brows drew together. "It's starting to freak me out. Nurses are cozying up to me in the scrub room, stopping me for a casual conversation in the hall. Even some of the managers are calling my cell with stupid questions."

Selena blinked. "I know how that feels but I suppose it's worse for a physician."

"A doctor of child-rearing age on the loose? It's open season and I hate it. This is a stupid thing to ask and let me know if I'm way off base, but could you be my pretend girlfriend?"

She cringed. "Don't know if I like the sound of that. Is that like friends with benefits?"

"Not at all. I mean, could you be my pretend new girlfriend? We go out a couple times, let the word leak that we're seeing each other. You'd really be helping me out." The guy looked so desperate. What was she supposed to say? Her mind started working. There could be advantages in this for her too.

"But no benefits, right?"

There was that hesitation again. "Not that I wouldn't like to, but no. Like I said, I'm keeping my head on straight, or trying. I trust you."

She could be making a fool of herself but it wouldn't be the first time. "Sure, I'll be your pretend girlfriend for a while. You're right. It'll be a relief for me too."

Gary eased out a breath. "Terrific. Be prepared to have me pay attention to you."

"I'm ready. Just don't even think of sending me flowers or anything like that. Let's just be visible."

"No kisses in the halls?"

"No sessions in the sleep room with the door locked." She'd always liked his sense of humor.

"And Seth? Want me to clue him in?"

She snorted. "Heck no! That would defeat the whole purpose on my end."

He was laughing. "Let the games begin."

She extended a hand. "Do you feel as relieved as I do?"

"Absolutely."

Hmm. Had he held her hand a little longer than necessary? No matter, Selena started to strategize. She'd just found her plan B.

Chapter 11

Outside the cafeteria windows, the dogwood trees rattled in the wind. Well, what was left of them. An unexpected ice storm had snapped off branches. Selena knew just how that felt but didn't new growth come with spring? She stabbed a cucumber slice with a fork and looked up.

Loping toward her with his long-legged stride, Gary caused quite a stir. He skidded to a halt. "Seven thirty okay tonight?"

Across from her, McKenna stopped chewing.

"Perfect. See you then."

"Great. Later." Quick wink and Gary veered toward the physicians' dining room. Selena popped the cucumber into her mouth and almost choked when two nurses tried to catch his attention. Taking out his phone as if he had a call, Gary put his head down and kept walking. The women sent curious glances in Selena's direction. For a second, all she heard was her own careful crunching and the distant chatter of employees.

"You going to tell me what that's all about?" McKenna finally asked.

"Nothing much. Just going to a movie." That much was true.

"Ah, hah. And when did all this start?"

"Ease up, okay? Nothing's really started."

McKenna wasn't buying it. "Gary's been pretty happy lately. You the reason?"

Thank goodness Selena's phone went off. It was the ER. "Brody, what's up?"

"Get your birthing gloves on. One of your patients just came in. Patty Lightcap. Looks like she's going to be a mama today."

"Tell her I'll meet her in the birthing suite." Ending the call, Selena stood up.

"Just like that, you're leaving?" Disbelief raised McKenna's voice.

She owed Seth's sister more than this. After all, she'd met Seth through McKenna. Still, that was one reason not to say too much. "This is a trial balloon, okay?"

"What are you talking about?"

"Gary. Hard to explain." Grabbing her tray, Selena practically ran to the rotating tray trolley. By the time she reached the hallway outside the birthing suite, Patty was being trundled toward her in a wheelchair. Keeping pace next to her, husband Jeremy looked pale.

"How far apart are your contractions?"

"Four minutes." Patty tensed but she got hold of the pain. Her husband massaging her shoulders, she panted until the contraction eased.

"Good girl." Selena opened the door and the orderly pushed Patty into the suite. "Now Jeremy, if you'll just help me."

But Patty stepped out of the wheelchair herself and slid onto the exam table. It didn't take long for Selena to assess the situation. "Perfect. All systems are go. Have you brought your music?"

Jeremy handed her a tape and she popped it into the CD player kept in the room. Like all the other couples, Patty and Jeremy had chosen their music during their natural childhood childbirth class as a part of their birth plan. Jeremy helped his wife into the shallow birthing pool.

Squatting in the water in her pink sports top, Patty nodded. Excitement glowed in her eyes. But the wave of love passing between husband and wife nearly swamped Selena. Shared commitment. Shared excitement. With every breath, Jeremy was with Patty. For the next two hours the young woman labored, her husband right there with her. At last, they reached the final phase. Checking the observation viewing panel, Selena smiled. "I see sandy hair, Patty. Big breath and one more push when the next contraction comes."

A Bach concerto and two loving parents welcomed Dylan Jeremy Lightcap into the world. "Will you just look at him?" Jeremy whispered to Patty when Selena handed her the tiny infant.

"Handsome like his daddy."

Blinking back her own tears, Selena handed the scissors to the new father. "Want to do the honors?" After Jeremy cut the cord, the pediatric nurse quickly took the infant to the heated bassinette while Selena and Patty worked on expelling the afterbirth.

An afternoon like this made her even more proud to be a part of the team. Hopefully by the time Selena had her own children, that new unit would be in place. The tug on her heart told her that she was ready. The tears in her eyes reminded her it wouldn't be easy.

"Ready to go up to the room?" Baby back in her arms, Patty nodded. A nurse had arrived from the obstetrics floor and the happy couple disappeared down the hall, blissful smiles on their faces.

When Selena reached the For Women office, patients crowded the waiting area. With three midwives busy in the practice, a birth during the day could put their schedule behind. Hustling back to her office, Selena checked her phone messages. Two were from Seth and she put them aside. Returning three of the other calls only took her about ten minutes. Then she hustled to catch up with patient appointments.

She loved her work here at Montclair and had been thrilled when McKenna recruited her. But sometimes she wished she'd never met McKenna's brother.

Hours later, Selena had seen her last patient and was dreaming of a hot soak in lavender epson salts.

"Busy day? Everything go all right with Patty?" McKenna stood in her doorway, Logan's ring glittering on her left hand.

"Cutest little baby boy ever. So how's your day? Why don't you take a seat?"

The caned seat of the rocker squeaked as McKenna sat down. Pushing with her white clogs, she began to rock. "Day went great, everything but lunch. One of my friends gave me indigestion."

"That'll happen."

The rocking stopped. "Look, I may be Seth's sister but you're a close friend. I know you're having a hard time, Selena, and I want to help."

Picking up a pen, Selena began to doodle on the pink phone messages from Seth. "I just don't want to put you in an awkward position."

"I'm a big girl. Try me."

Selena had to approach this with some delicacy. "Gary's in a similar situation, that's all. He and Mindy broke up."

"So I heard. What does that have to do with you?"

"I like Gary," Selena hurried to explain, "but more as a friend than anything else."

McKenna rolled her eyes. "I can hardly believe you're saying that. The man is so hot. If it weren't for Logan, I'd be on Gary Rice like tar on the Dan Ryan."

"You have a point. However, this break with Seth is very new and it's not something I'm going to get over fast." Selena's right hand kept working on those doodles.

Lifting up on her elbows, McKenna looked down pointedly at Selena's scribbles. She smiled when Selena drew a line through the hearts. "So you're going out with Gary as a friend? Comforting each other?"

"Sort of. We're dating...kind of."

"Can't wait to tell Seth."

Selena's pulse picked up. "Please don't. Dating someone so soon seems mean. After all, Seth hasn't done anything. Not really."

McKenna's tawny brows pinched together. "Isn't that the problem? He just hasn't done anything."

The two of them probably looked thick as thieves when Bethany stuck her head in. "What's up? Planning to rob a bank or something?"

Selena and McKenna exchanged a look. Outside, a March wind beat against the heavy paned windows.

Bethany waved a hand between the two of them. "Not saying anything? You both look guilty as sin. I'm out of here." She left.

"Back to business," McKenna said after their colleague's footsteps had retreated down the hall. "Couldn't be that you and Gary are working at making Seth jealous? You wouldn't stoop that low, right?"

"Not intentionally." Her defense came quickly.

McKenna's eyes grew thoughtful. "I don't know what will work with Seth. I really don't."

"Seth might not like this...macho pride and everything. But he'll start to date soon too." A mental image of women lined up outside Seth's house came to mind.

"I'm here to help. Where you headed tonight?"

"Gary suggested a movie at the Music Box Theatre. Then we'll probably hit Sluggers. I could go for a few pinball machines right now." Selena flexed her fingers and McKenna smiled. "Much better than slamming my head into a wall, right?"

"Got that right, girlfriend." Checking the time on her phone, McKenna jumped up. "Logan's waiting for me. We're going to the Purple Frog for a bite. I'd ask you to come if you didn't have a date. Or, a date that's not really a date."

"Not a date. Not really." Selena just couldn't go there, not yet.

"Right. Whatever." McKenna gave her a thumbs up before disappearing.

Packing up the stuff she wanted to take home, Selena figured that McKenna might get on the phone to Seth tonight. Nothing she could do about it. Part of her wanted Seth to know but the other part didn't want to deal with it. Hanging out with Gary might be just the medicine she needed.

When she got home, she started to draw a tub. After it was just the right temperature, she slipped into the lavender scented water for a relaxing soak. Aromatherapy was part of their natural childbirth classes and Selena was all for it. Lathering her skin with the softest aloe soap she could find, she was determined to give herself some of the self-care they taught in their childbirth class. She'd been through worse than this breakup with Seth, hadn't she?

Memories from her childhood flashed through her head, especially her farming days. Cutting her foot open by stepping on a rake. A snake bite in Fred Polk's orchard. Although he couldn't afford it, her father always insisted on getting care. One time the family had gone three days eating only white bread and root soup until payday arrived. All their money had paid for the doctor. Reserves were nonexistent. Her parents never even had a bank account.

Yep, she was darn tough and she could make it through heartache. Felt way worse than the rake, though. The metal art work she'd bought in Savannah had arrived. Just looking at those free flying birds made her heart sing. She'd hang it up this weekend.

Jumping out of the tub, she toweled off and applied her favorite gardenia-scented cream before taking inventory of her closet. With

Seth, she always wore something sexy. That's just how Seth rolled. When she opened that door, she wanted to see his dark eyes heat with approval. Gary? She'd practice on him. Finally, she decided on a black mini skirt with tights and her new boots. Her fuzzy gray turtleneck should keep her warm. The theater would be cold but Sluggers could heat up on a Friday night. After applying minimal makeup, she dressed and pulled on her boots.

Although she felt all cozied up in her turtleneck, the look in Gary's eyes when she opened the door made her feel like she was encased in clear plastic wrap. "Well, look at you." His eyes lit up although he kept his hands in his pockets when he stepped inside. The cold night air followed him, and Selena shut the door quick against a winter that refused to loosen its hold.

He sniffed and smiled. "I'm a sucker for sexy perfume."

She gulped. "Thanks. Let me get my jacket."

After she locked up, they started out. He kept a tight hold of her elbow on the way to his jeep. "You're quite the gentleman."

"Just what I do for all my girlfriends," he cracked, opening the passenger door.

"But I'm not..."

He held up one gloved hand. "Relax, Selena. Just kidding."

Fifteen minutes later, they were in the Music Box Theatre, munching buttered popcorn and taking in the latest Iron Man flick. Lots of action up on that screen but her heart wasn't in it. And Gary? He didn't laugh at the funny parts. With a sigh, she sat back and shoveled in more popcorn. When he didn't try to take her hand or loop one arm casually over her shoulder, she relaxed. The boundaries felt comfortable.

"Where to?" he asked as they left the theater.

"Thought we were going to Sluggers?"

He seemed to give himself a shake. "Right. Perfect."

Really? Poor guy. She tugged at his jacket. "Listen we don't have to..."

"No, no. Sorry. I'm just tired." He maneuvered her back to the car.

Basically a sports bar with plenty of screens, Sluggers had a second floor filled with games. Selena had to shout to be heard above the pinball machines. Chimes rang and balls thumped. And then there was the batting cage. Every crack of the bat made Selena feel better. The Black Hawks ice hockey game? She'd become an expert.

"You're killing me!" Gary complained, feverishly working the levers on his end.

"Three brothers. They would plead with my parents for just one game and that always had to be ice hockey." No need to explain that her family learned how to play in the back room of a bar owned by one of the farmers. Didn't cost him anything and the workers loved it. Ice hockey wasn't real popular down in Juarez, but learning the game had been fun up in *El Norte*.

Since Seth had an ice hockey game in his basement, she'd had plenty of practice as an adult. Seth and his brothers had whacked the heck out of it, and all his nieces and nephews learned to play at an early age.

But she didn't want to think about Seth tonight.

Gary sent the puck flying. Lights lit up and the bells clanged.

"No way." Selena bent to the task. At least these levers were something she could control. Her non-date looked on, his expression a mixture of awe and amusement.

"Whew, you gave me a run for my money," Selena said later as they went back downstairs.

"You're being polite, right? You whipped the pants off me."

They took two stools at the bar. As she sat down, Selena thought she saw a flash of dark auburn hair and darn it, her eyes swung to the end of the bar.

But it wasn't Seth. Just another tall, well-built guy with dark red hair.

"You checking someone out? You're on a date, remember?" Gary gave her a good-natured nudge.

Heat rolled up Selena's cheeks. "I'm sorry."

"Don't be. The good thing about being with you, Selena, is that we don't have to worry about the usual stuff. If you're interested in someone, well, I'd almost be happy for you. Feel kind of bad about involving you in this charade."

She frowned. "Don't be silly. I agreed to this and I am not checking out other guys."

"Aw, Selena." His arms muscular arms felt good when he hugged her. "I'm glad. Tonight I want to be your center of attention."

A party in the back broke into a loud "Happy Birthday" and Selena leaned closer to his ear. "What did you say?"

Brushing her hair aside, Gary repeated the message.

Nodding, Selena squeezed his arm. He was such a great guy.
"I'm good with that."

Caramba, she really was seeing things tonight. From the corner
of her eye, she thought she detected another flash of copper hair. A
girl's mind could play tricks on her when she had it bad for a man.

~.~

What was Gary doing, moving in on Selena like that? The beer mug
almost shattered in Seth's tight grip. And Selena. Was she cuddling
up with him? Sure looked like it. Seth liked Gary. Wasn't that the
rub? After all, the doc worked with Logan, McKenna's future
husband.

But he didn't like seeing Gary with Selena. From now on, he
had to ignore McKenna when she dropped her not-so-subtle hints.
Damn, felt like he was stalking his ex-girlfriend. Share his private
past with her? No way. He shoved the beer aside and threw some
bills on the bar. The last thing he wanted was for Selena to see him.

Marching out to his car, he slid in and sat there for a second. So
freezing cold out, he could see his breath in the air. He turned up
the heat but only cold air blasted his face. When would April get
here? Spring always came late to Chicago. Maybe he should take a
trip. Get out of town. Mexico or one of the islands.

Frustrated beyond belief, he shoved the car into gear. Who was
he kidding? If he went anywhere, he'd want Selena with him. Her
body stretched out next to his on the beach. Selena playing footsie
with his toes in the sand until he had to drag her back to the room,
not that she wasn't willing. Best girlfriend he'd ever had.

Girlfriend? Is that what she'd been? The word didn't feel like enough. No wonder Selena had it with him.

When he got on the Dan Ryan, he called McKenna.

"Why are you calling me so late?" He heard the yawn in her voice. "We're about to go to bed."

"Sorry." He glanced at the clock. Was he crazy? Getting enough sleep wasn't easy for a midwife. "Listen, did you casually mention Selena would be at Sluggers tonight for a reason? Is she dating Gary now? Didn't take her long."

Not long at all since he'd picked her up at O'Hare and they'd made love.

Love, not sex.

"Well, you'll have to ask her about Gary, won't you?"

He hated being put on the spot like this, and by his own sister. "Go back to sleep. Sorry if I woke you up. You going to Mom's Sunday?"

"Planning on it."

"Good. See you there." He ended the call.

Sunday. Another family dinner. When would he get used to family events without Selena, the girl all the Kirkpatricks adored?

And that included him.

When he pushed open the back door of his house and tossed his keys on the counter, Shadow was right there. "You waiting for me? That's nice, girl." Shrugging out of his jacket, he hung it up and went to check her bowls in the kitchen. "Had enough to eat?"

Suddenly hungry, he opening his refrigerator and grabbed some cold lasagna left over from last week's takeout. He'd been ordering out a lot. Just needed a fork. Soon as he sat down with his food,

Shadow leapt onto the stool next to him. "You women," he told his new pet between bites. "You don't know what you do to us."

Stretching toward the food, Shadow sniffed, one dainty paw up on the counter. His mother would have a fit and so would Selena. Good thing they weren't here.

"Always asking for something." But he smiled and grabbed a paper towel. After he forked a hunk onto the small sheet, he slid it over. Shadow didn't need any encouragement. Whiskers twitching, she was all over it.

"Good. You're my date for tonight." Seth kept eating.

"So how do I tell Selena how I feel about her? Huh, Shadow? What are the magic words here?" But would he be able to say them? To get them out?

The lasagna was gone. One whisk of her tail and his sounding board disappeared.

"Sure. Get what you want and walk away. Doesn't matter that I'm sitting here, a major mess." His words echoed in the silent kitchen. Why was it that he had no trouble talking about personal matters when he was alone?

Chapter 12

No roast this Sunday. Instead, the smell of turkey filled his parents' house. Seth set down the large cardboard box and hung up his jacket. Rearing up on her tiny legs, Shadow meowed, probably ticked that she couldn't see over the top. Or maybe the turkey smell was driving her nuts.

"Just be a good girl, okay?" Maybe bringing her had been another one of his bad ideas. He'd had a hard time fitting the litter box into the carton.

"Seth. Good, I need some help." His mother bustled out from the kitchen, eyes widening as she came closer. "Whatever do you have?"

"Shadow, meet Mom."

"Oh, my goodness. Where did you get him?"

"It's a girl. You could say she found me. That night after Mick's wedding? She was just sitting next to the dumpster. Crying. Starving."

"The poor little thing. She's beautiful." The kitten promptly rolled over so Reenie could stroke her belly. "Will you listen to that purring? Wait'll the kids see this."

"Is this okay? Kind of hated to leave her alone because I'm gone so much."

"No worries. It's fine." Reenie scooped Shadow up. The kitten's claws clung to his mother's sweater. "You'll have to have her declawed."

"Isn't that kind of mean?" He hated the thought of subjecting the little thing to surgery. But his furniture was taking a beating, especially the black leather sofa.

His mother planted a kiss on his cheek. "That's what I love about you, son. Soft-hearted, in a good way. Put the box in the corner of the kitchen, okay?"

Seth followed his mother back into the kitchen and stowed the box away. Talking baby talk all the way, Reenie settled Shadow back inside and nodded to a pile of silverware on the counter. "Now, wash your hands and then set the table, okay, honey? The girls are all busy with the kids. And the boys are watching the game. It'll just take you a minute."

"Yep. I can do that." When they were growing up, his mother had insisted that the boys shared the chores, whether it was doing the dishes or setting the table. He didn't mind it, although he never could remember which way the knife blade should face.

"Did I leave a burping cloth in here?" Amanda poked her head in.

Looking around, Seth lifted his shoulders. "Not that I can see. Morning sickness getting any better?"

She wrinkled her face. "Don't even ask."

"When's that due date again?"

"August, if I make it. Logan says we shouldn't be surprised if the twins come early." But Amanda didn't look panicked. She looked pleased.

"Think you're going to make it to McKenna's wedding?"

"Nope. Can't take any chances. But Connor's going. I can hold
the fort with Sean for a weekend." Her eyes traveled to the family
room where Connor was being all cutesy with Sean on the sofa.

"Don't worry. I'll take pictures," Seth assured her with a hug.

Amanda looked around. "Selena still missing in action?"

This was like taking a punch to the gut. "Yep. We're still taking
a b-break."

Shadow's pathetic wail reached him. "Sorry." He dashed back
into the kitchen with Amanda right behind him.

"Your cat's not happy," his mom told him.

"What have we here?" Amanda drew closer.

"Meet Shadow."

Amanda peered into the box. "I didn't know you liked cats."

"I'm learning." The turkey sat in its pan at the back of the
stove. Taking a knife, Seth sliced off some small bits and fed them
to the cat. "Now, be good. Hear me?"

Shadow licked her chops and curled up in the corner.

His sister-in-law trailed him into the dining room where he
finished up with the silverware. "So tell me more about this break
from Selena?"

"What? You and Connor never took time apart from each
other?" Didn't he just wish this was a temporary break. Selena had
him so confused. Add hurt and anger to that, if he were being
honest.

"No, we never took a break." Silly smile on her face, Amanda ran one hand over her stomach. "Sounds like an excuse to me. What's going on, Seth?"

This felt like an ambush and Seth didn't like it. "I think M-mom's calling me."

He escaped but his sister-in-law's frown followed him into the kitchen where his mother was still stirring the gravy. "Thanks, Seth." She grabbed a towel and patted her brow and neck.

"Is Shadow behaving?" Everything seemed quiet in the box.

"Fine. Guess the turkey made her sleepy." Usually his mother's face was flushed from the heat in the kitchen. But today she looked pale. Why hadn't he noticed that earlier? Sometimes his medical background made him hyper-vigilant.

With a shake of her head, she shushed him toward the door. "Don't stand there looking at me like that. I'm just fine now. I'll call you when the gravy's ready, okay? You worry too much." At least she wasn't pestering him about Selena. In fact, his mother seemed preoccupied.

Most of the gang was in the back and Seth was headed that way when McKenna barged through the front door, slammed it shut and unzipped her green jacket.

"Hey, McKenna. Where's Logan, my future brother-in-law?" Taking her jacket, Seth hung it up on the coat tree.

"Delivering a baby. He might not make it today, but I can take a doggie bag for him." McKenna's eyes searched his face and Seth turned away. "So what did you do last night? I mean after you called me?"

"Nothing much. W-why?"

Arms around his shoulders, McKenna pulled close and whispered, "Because I care about you, you big lug. Isn't that enough reason?"

But he hated this touchy-feely stuff and pushed away. "Don't tell me stuff about Selena, okay?" He intended to handle this himself.

"Did you call her today and ask her why she was at Slugger's with Gary?" His sister looked almost pleased.

"I don't like seeing Selena with Gary but there you have it." The words tasted like tin on his tongue.

"Gary's a great guy."

"Of course he is. He's a *doctor.*"

"Whoa." McKenna's hands shot out. "What does that have to do with anything? He's got his head on straight."

"Are you saying I don't?" She was being so damn irritating today.

"Just sounded like you were holding a grudge against doctors. Speaking of which, when are you going to start paramedic training?"

"So many questions. Soon, okay? Maybe I like being an EMT."

McKenna wasn't buying it. "Fine, but you should start climbing the ladder."

"I'm not a fireman."

"You know what I mean." She gave him the look, like she was reloading. "I understand Gary just broke up with Mindy."

The harsh chuckle burned his throat. "You don't say. Wonder why. Maybe he's got a c–com—"

"Commitment problem?" Throwing her head back, McKenna unleashed a hearty chuckle. "You can't even say the word? Really?"

"Their problems don't have anything to do with me."

"But you saw Gary with Selena. That doesn't concern you?"

She'd stumped him. Too many words tumbled in his head and he could not make sense of them. Not today.

A roar went up from the family room. He'd rather be back there watching a game than here getting the first degree.

But McKenna was a pit bull today. "Sometimes couples need to evaluate their relationship."

"You sound like a therapist. " Maybe he needed one. Seth rubbed the back of his neck. Had he showered that day? Couldn't recall. Running a hand over his chin, he realized he hadn't shaved either. What was happening to him? Folding his arms tight across his chest, he casually angled away from his sister.

"How do you feel about having Easter at your house?"

"Mom always has Easter." He could almost smell the ham roasting now.

"Time for a change. My place is too small and the others have kids."

"Joe doesn't have kids."

"He lives in a two-bedroom apartment, Seth. What's the problem? You have Nascar parties at your place all the time." Impatience crackled in McKenna's voice.

It almost pleased him to get her riled after what she'd put him through. But maybe he was making too much out of this. "Sure, all right. I'll have Easter. It'll keep me busy. "

That tsking thing that McKenna did annoyed him. If anyone knew what was going on with Selena, it was McKenna. But she wasn't sharing. "Do you need to be kept busy?"

He swallowed hard. "You know what? That was your last shot. Time to carve the turkey." His boots squeaked on the hardwood floors, he turned so fast.

Head pulsing with annoyance, he found his mother rubbing Big Mike's back in the kitchen. Stopped Seth in his tracks. This was how Mom acted with his dad when the squad lost someone in a fire. Or when a baby was late.

So, what was wrong now? A chill chased up his spine.

Ten feet away but he picked up his mother words. "Now, Mike. It's probably nothing. I'm going to have the tests and we'll see."

Not what a son likes to hear. Seth stepped into the room. "What tests? What'll be fine?"

Looking uncomfortable, his parents sprang apart. Reenie nudged Big Mike with an elbow and his dad's face reddened. "Might as well tell him, Mike. The rest should know too, one by one. No group drama, please."

When his mom tossed her head like that, she was the same feisty redhead he remembered growing up. The woman who could wave her potato masher in his face and threaten "consequences" if he didn't clean up his room.

But his father opened and closed his mouth. No words. How often did that happen? Seth turned back to his mom. "Okay, tell me. Now."

His mother pushed a wisp of graying hair from her face. "I'm going to have some tests next week. That's all."

Seth's chest tightened. "What kind of tests?"

She gave him that shoulder roll that told him this was none of his business. But it was. "Just growing older stuff. Normal stuff."

Tests weren't used for "normal stuff." They were ordered for abnormal stuff, suspicious stuff. Seth pushed on. "You having the tests done at Montclair?"

His mom nodded. "McKenna knows all about it and we'll tell the rest of the family...in time. Everything will be fine. You're in healthcare and you know that."

"You've been talking to McKenna but not me?" When had his sister become the authority on everything?

"Everything's fine, son." Big Mike stepped in front of Seth's mom, but she gently pushed him aside.

"Yes, it is and that's why you should go back to watch the game, Mike. You too, Seth."

Big Mike could handle just about anything. Now he shuffled from the room, like he'd been sent out of the game. Seth stayed. His mother went back to stirring the gravy. The sun came through the window above the sink and it could have been any old Sunday. But the questions percolating in Seth's mind needed answering. Was this why McKenna suggested he have Easter?

"How about I have Easter at my house?"

Frowning, his mother brought the wooden spoon to her mouth, blew on the steaming gravy and tasted. Grabbing the salt, she sprinkled a liberal dose over the wide, flat pan, then stopped and smacked her forehead. "Pepper not salt, Maureen."

Picking up the pepper she sucked in a breath. "That's awful nice, Seth. Might take you up on that."

A cold fist closed over his heart. The old Reenie would have waved that spoon at him and said, "Fiddlesticks. We always have Easter here."

"Yep, sounds fine, son." She kissed him on the cheek. "That's really sweet."

Seth's concern mounted. "So what kind of test?"

"Oh, just checking out a lump. Nothing much." She kept up with the pepper. "So what's going on with Selena?"

Geez. His mother was an expert at evasion. "I already told you, M-mom. Nothing."

The disappointment in her eyes killed him. "You haven't fixed that yet? And could your mother ask why?"

God it was hot in here. "Life happens, Mom."

"When are you going to settle down, Seth, huh? Have your own family?" His mother looked as confused as he felt.

He had no answer. Family was important to the Kirkpatricks. "Settling down isn't that simple."

"It isn't?" His mother put down the wooden spoon. "What's complicated about it?"

He sure as heck couldn't explain and didn't want to bring it up. How would his mother feel if she knew he didn't have a clue how to dazzle Selena, not with words. She'd tried so hard to make everything right for him. Special tutors, speech therapists. All at a cost they couldn't afford.

Seth's knees almost buckled with relief when Malcolm appeared in the door. "Are we going to eat soon, Mom? Kids are hungry and..." His words drifted off. "Am I interrupting something?"

"Almost there, Malcolm, okay?" A shake of her head and his mother was back in Sunday dinner mode. Malcolm disappeared.

But the questions about Selena had cinched a painful band around Seth's chest. He wanted to feel her arms around his waist, wanted to smell her light flowery perfume, be tickled by the soft hair under his chin when she cuddled close. Wanted to see her hands flutter in the air while she talked and talked. She was always so good at filling the silences.

"Don't just stand there, Seth," his mother scolded. "Carve the turkey, would you? Time to get this meal on the table."

Grateful for the distraction, he got to work. After he'd helped his mother bring out the platters of turkey, green beans and parsleyed new potatoes, they all gathered at the long table. Dishes were passed around. Conversations bounced off the walls. Seth could hardly stomach either one. His appetite was definitely off and he picked at his meal. Lisa, Malcolm's three year-old daughter, sat on one side of him and usually he loved to tease her. Halfway through the meal she sniffed and said, "You smell funny, Uncle Seth."

Across the table, Dana, Lisa's mother, gasped. "Lisa Maureen, you say you're sorry."

Of course, his siblings roared. Was it hot in here or was he blushing? As if that wasn't enough, on the other side of him Mick, Lisa's brother, mumbled, "He does smell funny, Dad."

Perfect. Just perfect.

The concerned glances from Seth's parents at the end of the table made eating even more challenging. He was trying to figure out an excuse to leave when Lisa piped up again.

"Something's pulling at my jeans! Oh, look. Will you just look?"

She got to Shadow before Seth could and had the kitten in her arms at the table, a definite no-no. "No pets at the table." His mother's look was thunderous.

In all the confusion, he grabbed Shadow and made an escape. The kitten was pissed when she got plunked back into the box. He'd have to get a carrier. If he'd been thinking the cat was temporary, he was kidding himself.

"You're a lot of trouble, you know that?" Shadow's blue eyes peeked at him over the top edge of the carton he'd set under the heat vent below the dashboard. "You women are always trouble."

She gave a screeching meow that probably meant *Deal with it.*

At home, he got Shadow settled and then headed straight for the shower. The soap in the holder was dry, never a good sign. And he was the neatnick of the family. But while he sudsed his hair, all he could think about was the last time Selena had joined him, shampooing his hair with her long nails. His scalp tingled, remembering. When she'd slowly soaped his body, one inch at a time, he thought he'd drown. Now he turned the knob until the water felt like ice cubes. Bowing his head, he let the water pummel him until he couldn't stand it anymore. Then he turned it off, jumped out and grabbed a towel.

Hair still damp, he decided to clean his family room. Like his parents' house, the room had been added after he bought the place.

His brothers and dad had helped, while his mom cooked chili in the kitchen. That chili. Selena had asked his mom for the recipe. Battling memories, he cleaned up the newspapers and then hauled out the vacuum. Shadow disappeared.

Two weeks out from Easter and he wanted the house to shine. Maybe he'd get the windows cleaned. No matter if they had four inches of snow on the lawn, somehow he had to have an egg hunt for the kids on Easter.

Grabbing a pen and paper, he began to make a list. He always had to write things down. In the quiet kitchen, he could almost hear Selena teasing him. *"Mi amor,* what are you doing?" She would take the pad from his hand and add a few things. He'd never minded, as long as he ended up with a list to check off.

Now he wondered if McKenna had told Selena. Had she explained why he needed lists? Funny, that hadn't occurred to him before. Was his sister sharing personal stuff that would embarrass him?

For a second, something that felt like the flu consumed him. He slumped onto one of the stools at the kitchen counter. Maybe he was coming down with something. "Forget it, Kirkpatrick," he told himself. The brush of Shadow's tail made him jump. Grabbing the cat, he ruffled her fur. "You women are all alike. Trouble. Even the ones we love. And maybe that's why we love you."

The thought stopped him cold.

His hands tightened on the cat. With an angry snarl, she jumped down.

He loved Selena. Loved her. That realization came back to

mock him, only this time it felt bigger. Huge. The future unwound in his head like a bumpy road he had to smooth out. How would he tell her? What would he say?

Seth grabbed a pen and paper.

Chapter 13

Four days later, Selena sat with McKenna in the women's center at Montclair Specialty Hospital, anxiety skittering through her stomach. Selena loved Reenie, just like she loved Reenie's son. Even if there were a problem, it had been caught in an early stage. McKenna had reassured her that Maureen had been like clockwork about her mammograms.

While she was worried about Maureen, she was also concerned about Seth. Although the men in the Kirkpatrick family looked strong as oak trees, they had their weaknesses. Their mother topped the list, especially for Seth.

Selena's clinic appointments didn't start for an hour. She wanted to be here with McKenna but fidgeted in the vinyl seat. The waiting room smelled like coffee but if Selena had one more cup, she'd jump out of her skin. Across from her, McKenna paged through a magazine. Big Mike was with his wife during the minimally invasive breast biopsy "How's your dad taking this?"

"Not well." Tossing the magazine aside, McKenna must have seen the question in Selena's eyes. "Seth isn't taking it too good either. Oh sure, he seems to be. Keeps getting his house ready for Easter. Last I knew he was up on the roof hammering shingles."

"In this weather? Isn't it icy up there?"

"You tell him that. Oh I forgot. You're not speaking to him." McKenna gave Selena a tired smile.

Selena's throat thickened. Why was she even here? She'd broken up with the guy. But the truth was, Seth's mom felt like her own *mamacita* and McKenna, another sister. When you break up with a man, you break up with his family too. The big hurt, two times over. Sitting here today, Selena felt shredded inside.

Overhead, the operator paged McKenna, who checked her phone and made a call. Selena slid down in her vinyl seat. The hands of the big clock on the wall seemed stalled. Hadn't it been seven fifteen an hour ago? Picking up the magazine McKenna had just discarded, Selena couldn't read a word. Her delivery the night before had lasted almost all night. Her head felt like a pumpkin and her eyes weren't focusing.

Or was it her heart making it hard to concentrate?

Seth's texts had fallen off and she missed them. If one more nurse asked her how it was going with Gary, she'd scream. Sure, Gary seemed perfectly happy with the arrangement. Women weren't pestering him anymore. But Selena? The time she spent with Gary felt empty. She missed the excitement of getting dressed for a date, the anticipation before she opened the door. Maybe she just missed Seth. Last time they grabbed a bite, all Gary did was talk about Mindy.

The door to the waiting room swung open. Selena's heart just about stopped. Was this haggard man with wild gray hair Big Mike? Looking up, he saw them. The broad shoulders swung back and he smoothed one hand over his thinning strands.

Too late. Selena had already seen the stress.

McKenna ended her call and turned to her dad. "How's Mom doing?"

"Everything's fine." Rubbing his hands together, Big Mike looked like he was gathering his thoughts. He rarely spoke off the cuff, just like his son. "Your mom's great. Procedure went well. We should have some results, ah, this afternoon." His bravado slipped. "I hope."

"More likely tomorrow, Dad. We have to be patient." McKenna gave her dad a Kirkpatrick hug, which was no small thing, arms tight and cheeks pressed together. "Even if the lab results come back positive, we got it early. Mom's a strong lady."

Selena didn't belong here. She felt like the puzzle piece that would never fit. This was definitely a time for family and she was intruding, mooning over the only man who could have made this feel right. McKenna and her father had their heads together. She was rubbing his back, the way her mother did.

"See you all later." Turning, Selena stumbled toward the elevator, her white clogs squeaking on the tile floor. She punched the button for the third floor. Once the stainless steel doors whooshed closed, she dashed a finger under each eye. Time to snap out of it.

But her longing for Seth wouldn't allow it. If her work didn't keep her up at night, her own restlessness did. Weeks ago, she'd tucked her favorite picture of the two of them far back in her lingerie drawer. Last night, she'd brought it out when she got home. Arms around each other's waists, they looked so happy.

Propping the photo against a mug on the kitchen table, she raided her freezer and downed at least a half a pint of cherry chip ice cream.

She should throw that photo out.

Instead, she put it back on her dresser.

Once the elevator door opened, Selena sprinted across the overpass that spanned the street between the hospital and the medical office building. The For Women office was bustling when she came through the door. "Here you go, Selena." Dorothy handed her a sheaf of pink phone messages. Head down, Selena trudged back to her office and began to return calls.

When McKenna finally came back from the hospital, there was no need to ask. "My dad's hoping for test results today but they probably won't be back until tomorrow, at the earliest."

Selena wanted to call Seth. He must be *loco* right about now. But she didn't.

Intruder. The word echoed in Selena's mind until she blocked it by repeating the words from one of Adele's songs.

Easy to straighten out her thoughts, but she couldn't help her heart. *That* was with Seth Kirkpatrick. Was he hurting now, too?

When Gary asked her if she wanted to stop for something to eat after work, she said no, way too preoccupied to be cheery. That night she hardly slept. After lunch the next day, McKenna appeared in her doorway. Selena knew from the look on her face, the news wasn't good.

Her friend slumped into the chair across from Selena's desk.

"So it was positive?"

McKenna nodded. Strange to see her friend so dazed.

"McKenna," she ventured, "Maureen isn't my mom, but you know this is treatable and very early, from what you've said."

Her friend gave her head a shake, like she was trying to clear it. "In my head, I know all that. But this stuff happens to other people. When it happens to you, it feels weird."

"Surgery?"

"Right, in a couple of days. Dad asked me to spread the word. He does not want to do it, so I have to call my brothers and Harper. Keep them all from freaking out."

What about Seth? Selena chewed on the corner of her lip.

"Mom wants it all behind her." McKenna broke into Selena's spinning thoughts. "Wants to be ready for Easter, even though Seth is having it."

"So you said. Is this why?" The hole inside her grew wider.

McKenna nodded. "We figured it would be better."

How would Seth ever take care of all the details? No big deal to stick a ham in the oven, and the women would help bring the side dishes. But Easter entailed more than food. Reenie always had blow-up bunnies for the kids, an egg hunt outside, decorations galore. How would Seth handle the little touches that made the day special? Picturing him making one of his lists, Selena shuffled papers on her desk. "I'm sure he'll be fine."

"But you still worry about him? Maybe because you should be with him?"

"No, no. I'm fine. I wanted this."

"And I encouraged you." McKenna blew out a sigh. "Oh,

honey. If this is not what you want, raise your hand. I feel terrible. I'm sure Seth wouldn't mind if you came. Your own folks are in Kalamazoo. Usually you don't go home for Easter."

Time to draw a line. "I wouldn't even think of going to Seth's. Right now, I have a patient waiting." She made a show of checking her phone and McKenna left.

The next few days were rough. Maureen's surgery went fine. She chose a lumpectomy and needed no further treatment right now. Like the trooper that she was, Seth's mother put it all behind her. When Selena stopped in Reenie's room to say hello the day of the surgery, the room was packed with family. Connor was there, along with Malcolm and yes, Seth. They joked with her and for a second it felt just like old times.

But it wasn't.

Every time she looked up, Seth's dark eyes burned holes in her. Was he angry with her? Or was he hurting?

Sure, she'd chosen this separation because she got tired of waiting. Now she was having second thoughts. Three days later, Gary poked his head into her office to ask if she wanted to stop for a drink after work. She pleaded off.

"What's this? You dumping me already?" he teased, lounging in her doorway with that sexy way he had.

"Not at all. I just have things to do."

Think I'll go home and stare at the picture of my old boyfriend.

If the man she loved was hurting, then she was hurting. And oh yes, it remained clear that she loved Seth. Loved his silly jokes, when he finally remembered the punch line, loved his sly, sexy looks, loved the way he cared about his family. This charade with Gary had gotten old.

"Listen, Gary..."

"So, you *are* dumping me."

The expression on his face made her chuckle. "Yes, and I don't think you care."

Shaking his head, Gary smiled. "Look, it was kind of a lame idea. You deserve better."

"You're a great guy. But I have to be true to myself."

"I understand." One eyebrow arched. "Besides Selena, if we kept at this, it would lead to something. You know that, right?"

She should have been flattered. "Maybe. But not with me."

"I admire your conviction. Any man would." Pursing his lips, her maybe-boyfriend pushed away from the doorframe. "Bye, girlfriend." With a wave, he was gone.

A wave of relief washed over her. She liked to keep her head straight and lately? Kind of muddled. Time to put on her big girl pants.

That night, Selena zipped to the locker room to shower and change clothes. Dressed in her tight jeans and a turtleneck, she spritzed herself with Seth's favorite perfume. After donning her silver jacket, she looped Seth's favorite green scarf around her neck and drove out to Oak Park. The heat blasting in her car couldn't stop her shivering inside.

Sometimes a girl's gotta do what a girl's gotta do.

But it's never easy.

The trip up the Dan Ryan and over the Eisenhower gave her

time to think. Not always a good thing. When she got to Seth's tidy brick house, she pulled up in front and sat there for a second. His lights were on and the jeep sat in the driveway. Her breath came in short gasps. When she cracked open her window, the March breeze held just a hint of spring. The weather had turned warmer and dry leaves rustled in the tall trees overhead. Suddenly too warm, she tugged off the bright green scarf.

But when indecision chipped away at her, she got out.

No way was she backing away. Her heart wouldn't allow it and she marched toward the door. Night still fell early and the street lamps had just come on. Coach lights glowed at either side of his door. Reenie always said the outside lights should be on at night so that everyone knew they were welcome.

When she reached Seth's front door, she sucked in some deep breaths. How often had she arrived breathless to see him? This time she didn't even kid herself that she was here as a friend. She was gunning for him, plain and simple. Selena's new Savannah boots stayed rooted to Seth's welcome mat. Beyond this door, he was hurting. She just knew it and that was the only thing pulling her forward. That and the enormous love she still had for him.

Glancing down, she spied the yellow and purple crocus peeking through the crusty brown of a flowerbed. *Un milagro de primavera.* She'd planted these with Seth last fall, so maybe not a spring miracle. Bought the bulbs on a whim. Now they smiled up at her like a good omen. A sign of spring and change.

Raising one hand, she hammered that bell. The deep chime rang clear through to her backbone. This might be a bad idea but it was full speed ahead.

When the door opened, Seth stood there, unbearably cute in a rumpled T-shirt and low slung jeans. Her eyes drank him in like a warm cup of coffee. But his glance turned wary and that hurt. She swayed.

He reached out to steady her. "Hey, ba-, ah, Selena."

He'd nearly said "Babe." A good sign.

Her body curved toward him. Selena wanted to tug that word from his lips like a magic silk scarf. Every cell in her body clamored for his words, the words he wouldn't say.

She moved ahead with her plan. "Just thought I'd stop by. Was in the neighborhood."

"Come on inside. It's freezing out there." Grabbing her hand, Seth pulled her into the warm hallway. She closed her fingers tight around his but once inside, he disengaged. Fine. Maybe her desertion after the airport was still too fresh.

A fire crackled in the living room fireplace and the smell of chili filled the air. She could taste the cayenne pepper on her tongue. He helped her off with her jacket. So hard not to shiver every time his hands brushed her shoulders.

"Had anything to eat?"

"Yep," she lied. "Grabbed something before I left the hospital."

But damn. The guy knew her so well. His eyes brushed her face before settling on her lips. "Mind keeping me company while I eat?"

"No. Of course not."

By this time they were in the long hallway leading to the

kitchen, a gauntlet of family pictures, including tons of weddings. One day, their picture would be there. She was determined.

The kitchen looked just the same, like she'd left it yesterday. Same rooster dish towels next to the sink, same red dinnerware set on the oval oak table with spindle chairs, same Chicago Bears magnets on his stainless steel refrigerator.

"Glass of wine?" Seth turned and his midnight eyes held her captive.

"Sounds good."

When he popped the cork, she heard a definite "meow."

"Ah, come on, Shadow. It's okay." Bending down behind the counter, he scooped up the tiny gray kitten.

"How's Shadow adjusting?"

"She runs the house."

Giving the cat a good scratch behind the ears, Seth said, "She's getting along fine, aren't you, girl?" The cat closed her eyes blissfully while Seth worked her with his gentle hands. How Selena envied that little kitten.

"Looks like she's found a good home."

"We get along." Putting the cat down, he reached for the wine bottle. "Red?"

She nodded. For a big guy, Seth had sensitive hands. She loved to watch them. Longed to feel them. But tonight worry slumped his shoulders. So much still had to be decided about Reenie.

I'm getting ahead of myself.

Seth poured the wine into two glasses while Selena's eyes drifted to the calendar hanging from his refrigerator. No way would she sneak a peek at any notes written on the weekend squares. She concentrated on his shifts. Late shift for the next two weeks. Excellent. When he handed her the goblet, she ran her fingers up the stem. Seth raised his glass. "To..."

"To spring coming soon." She clinked her glass to his. A narrow miss. They had always toasted each other. Well, she was prepared to wait.

"Let's sit down." He pulled out a chair and she sat. "So, is this a social call?"

"Uh, no. Yeah. I guess." *I'm making a mess of this.* "How are you?"

"Fine. Just great." The lines bracketing his lips, fanning from his eyes, told her that wasn't true.

"Your mom will come through this. You know that, right?"

He tilted his head to one side. "Kind of early but you're right. It's just that, well, I don't know, Selena. This is my mom."

She had to pick her way slowly through the minefield of his emotions to discover where he was. For a couple moments, they sipped. The atmosphere felt heavy with unsaid words. She glanced out the back window to the rope swing hanging listlessly from an oak tree. His nieces and nephews loved that swing. "Spring is coming soon.

Seth took a slow sip, leaving his bottom lip moist. "Yep, Easter's right around the corner."

"So I hear." She couldn't drop her eyes from that full lip.

"I'm having the family party here. You know, because of..." His eyes veered away.

"Of course." She'd always loved the noisy chaos of the Nascar or football parties he held in this house. Everyone brought something. Easter would be just like that. Chaotic and fun.

"What are you doing for Easter?"

"Nothing." No time to think of a good lie.

"Why don't you come on over? The family would love to see you."

Her mouth opened and closed, mind spinning.

"I mean, like a friend. Just come as a friend." His cheeks were flushing, like they were too close to the fireplace. They always liked to cuddle up there while the winter winds shrieked outside. Cozy. Exclusive. Her skinned burned, remembering. They'd done a lot more than just cuddle.

Tonight they were a million miles from that fireplace.

She'd take baby steps. "Sounds good. Sure. Thanks for the invitation."

His frown eased into a smile and he got up to stir his chili.

She'd come to lay some groundwork. Instead, she felt her own strength melting. Seth seemed so preoccupied. Probably worried about his mother. He just kept stirring his chili. "Maybe I'll just set another place?"

"Oh, no. I really have to go." She slid from the stool, leaving her half-full glass of wine. If she drank it, she might do something she'd regret. She didn't want to push him, not tonight.

No way was she falling off the wagon again, only to have nothing resolved.

"Sure you won't stay?" He looked alarmed. And nervous.

"No really, I'm, ah, meeting a friend at the Comeback Inn tonight." Tonight distance would be better. She needed to think.

"Oh, okay." The coziness melted from the room.

Seth was scowling when she said good night.

"What can I bring Easter to help?"

"Anything, I guess." He scrubbed one hand through his hair, leaving it upended. Her fingers prickled.

"Thought I might take care of the goodies for the kids."

"Goodies?" Such a guy. He looked totally perplexed.

"You know, *pequeñas cosas*." Her hands fluttered in the air and a smile tilted his lips. "Things your mother always has. Plastic bunnies, that kind of stuff."

"Right. Sure, that'll be great."

Helping her into her jacket, Seth let his hands rest on her shoulders. She felt his heat behind her. It would be so easy to spoon her body into his. Would he wrap his strong arms around her? But his body stiffened. Seth pushed away from her like a boat leaving the pier.

"Night, Selena. Thanks for stopping by."

The key to his house was in her purse. She'd meant to return it. Now she had a totally different plan for that key. Smiling, she slung the purse over her shoulder and left.

Chapter 14

Seth stood on his deck, surveying his back yard. Easter morning and things were looking pretty good. Only he didn't feel good. Not since Selena's visit. Sitting across from her, he'd wanted to say so much. But the words wouldn't come. Not the right words, anyway. Besides, she was on her way to meet Gary. Maybe that's the kind of guy she needed. Gary was never at a loss for words.

With a sigh, he pushed away from the handrail. Overhead, the oak trees were thick with red buds. One good rain and they'd bloom. About time. Clouds hung gray and heavy overhead and he hoped they held off until after the egg hunt. All the colored eggs McKenna had dropped off were hidden. He'd waited until morning to do that so the raccoons wouldn't find them first. A stack of yellow and green plastic buckets sat on the deck. Only five kids but the game would keep them busy for what, thirty minutes? He'd come home one day to find a huge bag of stuff tucked into the back storm door. Selena must have stopped and he felt sorry he'd missed her. But he got to work. Blew up the bunnies and scattered the paper decorations around this morning.

The big surprise came when two boxes arrived from Macys. The red dishes packed inside made him smile. Was this a peace omen from Selena? Arranging the dishes neatly in his dishwasher,

Seth knew it wasn't going to be this easy. Selena was a complicated woman. He wouldn't have her any other way.

But right now, he didn't have her.

And Easter was his one chance to get her back.

His shoulders ached from all the yard work this past week. Gave him less time to think about Selena and how bad he'd wanted her the night she stopped over. Just to feel her in his arms. Bury his nose in her thick hair. Feel her lips. Oh yeah, those lips. But what would he say? Her visit caught him by surprise so he had no time to think. No time to pull together the words that could win her back.

And she was meeting Gary. This felt like the chess game he could never master. He couldn't risk one more wrong move.

Sure, he'd taken her up on her offer to help on Easter. McKenna had mentioned that half the colored eggs were from Selena. But Seth wanted a lot more than a bunch of Easter eggs. Hands on the railing, he leaned forward and tried to convince himself that some of her was better than nothing.

That just didn't fly.

Truth was, he wasn't himself right now. Reenie's diagnosis had hit him hard and he couldn't shake it. The memory of that woman who didn't make it to the hospital in time haunted him. He'd never forget the look on her husband's face—like he'd lost everything.

Lately, he'd been stopping at his parents' house for dinner, bringing supper so his dad wouldn't try to cook. The only thing Big Mike could whip up was potato pancakes. He used way too much oil and nearly burned the house down one time. So Seth picked up chicken, burgers or pizza and took it to their house. "Go on, now," his mother told him after his third cup of coffee last Wednesday night. "All this carryout must be costing you a fortune. Don't you have a lot to do for Easter? I feel so bad that we couldn't have it here."

His dad shut that down fast. "Now, Reenie, it's time to let someone else do something for a change. You can hardly raise your arm, sweetheart." That was the truth. His mother was still recuperating from her surgery and his dad treated her as if she were made of glass.

It reminded him of a dream he'd had the other night. He was down on Navy Pier with Selena when a storm kicked up. All of a sudden she was swept away by high wind and waves. He'd jumped in but couldn't find her. Instead he sank down, down into the icy waters until he could not breathe. Until he was cold and floating.

The dream had been hard to shake off. He had plenty of good memories of Navy Pier with Selena, which made the nightmare strange. For her last birthday, they'd gone on one of the cruises around the harbor. The sky had been all stars and moonlight that night and Selena had whispered that it was the most romantic night ever.

The kind of night when a man proposes. But he hadn't proposed. In fact, it hadn't even occurred to him until his friend Brian brought it up. "Man, you popped for that cruise? That's where I proposed to Steffie. Time for the ball and chain, huh?"

Seth had just stared at his high school friend. Brian married Steffie and now they were expecting. He wanted to ask Brian what he'd said, how he'd proposed. But his friend would have a field day with that question.

Time to shake off his messed up life. Sure, he wished the sun would come out but that didn't seem likely. No leaves on the trees yet, but tulips were poking up in the back yard, replacing the crocus. He didn't go on duty until late tonight and if he were called out earlier, fine with him. The Kirkpatricks were used to men working odd hours. They'd just carry on.

Going back inside, he poured himself another cup of coffee. Shadow appeared from somewhere, sweeping her gray tail around Seth's ankles. "What do you want now, you little beggar? You've already had your breakfast." Cuddling her in his arms, he took her with him on a final check of the house. It felt good to have her softness in his arms.

The cat had taken to sleeping with Seth. He'd fixed a bed for her down in the kitchen but she wouldn't stay there. Too cold or too far away? She'd leap onto his bed after all the lights were out and cozy up next to him. Seth didn't have the heart to turn her out.

Setting Shadow on the black sofa, he reached for one of the huge pillows Selena had brought over months ago. Using both hands, he tried to plump it up the way she did. "Add some color to the place, *mi amor*," she'd told him. The red and purple pattern was so Selena. She knew how to brighten things up.

Something silky and purple caught his eye. Reaching down, he pulled out a pair of purple panties. His mind froze. He knew who they belonged to but how had they gotten here? He'd vacuumed this sofa the weekend before, just to get a jump on Easter. Shadow batted at the silky piece. "These are definitely not for you. You're too young." He stuffed them in his pocket. Time to go on a hunt. After all, the family was coming.

In the kitchen, he found a recipe for Selena's Mexican Chili, tucked in the top drawer of the desk. His pulse speeded. The dining room was next and he tore open drawers of the credenza Selena had found at a resale shop. Speared by a fondue fork were ticket stubs from a movie they'd seen together. "Such a sentimental girl, Shadow." The cat followed him from room to room.

Nothing was as personal as the first discovery but everything socked him right in the solar plexus. Why hadn't he noticed her purple toothbrush tucked in the drawer of the bathroom upstairs? Or her extra robe hanging in the back of his closet? He'd been walking about in a fog while Selena played this joke on him.

She was waving the green light. Maybe she wasn't so serious about Gary after all.

Forty minutes later, he was pretty sure that he had found everything. His heart thudded in his chest as he looked around. The house had become his project after he bought it three years earlier. He was proud of it and wanted it to look nice. After all, first time he'd had a holiday here. Nascar races and Bears games? Sure, but never a holiday. The place looked good. After everyone got here, it wouldn't make much difference. Fifteen minutes and the coffee table would have peanut shells on it and one of the kids would have spilled a soda on the carpet.

McKenna had stopped by earlier with two egg casseroles, along with directions. Amanda dropped off packages of hash browns and a huge bag of bagels. "I will be here to toast these and I'm bringing cinnamon butter. Don't worry about the sausage. I'm bringing it with me, already cooked."

Checking McKenna's directions, he turned the oven on and went to shower. As he soaped his body under the hot water, he knew Selena would show up. She wouldn't go to all this trouble for nothing.

Freshly showered and shaved, Seth grabbed some notes he'd made when he was clear-headed two nights ago. Folding the paper carefully, he tucked it in his pocket and headed downstairs. He was shaking the tomato juice for Bloody Marys when he heard people at the door.

"Happy Easter, Uncle Seth!" James and Randy, Mark's boys, raced into the kitchen, followed closely by their dad and his wife, Jamie.

"Happy Easter to you, too."

"Where's Shadow, Uncle Seth?" Randy asked.

"In the family room, last I checked. Just hold out your hand and wait for her to come to you. Don't grab or you'll scare her." Elbowing each other, the two boys disappeared.

"I'll just set this veggie tray on the buffet, Seth." Jamie swept past with a huge foil-covered tray.

"When's the Easter egg hunt?" Randy dashed back to ask, Shadow not looking too happy in his arms.

"As soon as everyone gets here. How about that?"

"Oh, boy! I'll beat you to the swings," Randy told his younger brother James, handing Shadow to Seth. The two boys scrambled to the back door.

"Trying to get a jump on the egg hunt," Mark told Seth in an undertone.

"No searching until I say so," he called after them.

"They're ruffians," he whispered to Shadow. She gave him a slow blink of her blue eyes, as if she agreed.

No such thing as arriving late with the Kirkpatrick family. Before long they were all present and accounted for, with his mother set up in the barcalounger in front of the TV, his dad fussing around her.

Watching his father bring his mom a mug of chicory coffee, Seth wondered.

"You sure Mom's okay?" he asked McKenna, who was unmolding her popular strawberry jello in the kitchen.

"Oh course she is."

Logan came by and kissed McKenna on the neck.

"That tickles!" McKenna giggled. "You'll make me drop the jello mold."

"How about this." Bending his head deeper, Logan aimed lower.

Too much PDA for Seth. "Okay none of that. You two are getting married soon. Can't you wait?"

"No. As a matter of fact, I can't." Logan gave Seth a sly smile. "Besides, I can't do this around the hospital."

"Lord, I hope not." When the two of them got mushy, Seth hardly knew what to do. "I think Mom's calling me."

Logan dropped the smile. "Your mother's going to be fine,

Seth. You know that, right?"

"Of course I do." Did Logan think Seth couldn't handle it? He filled another mug with coffee and carried it into the family room where Reenie was holding court.

When he reached his mother, three mugs were arranged on the TV table next to her. "Mercy me, honey. Do I look like a woman who could drink all this?" Mark, Malcolm and Connor had all gotten there before him. In the background, his dad hovered. Was he even watching the golf tournament on TV? His mom grabbed Seth's hand.

"Sure smells good in here, son. Maybe you should take over having this event for me."

Seth jerked and his coffee slopped over onto the gray carpet. "No way. Next year? You're back on."

"Maybe I like having my kids fuss about me." His mother nodded her head in Big Mike's direction. "Your father can certainly do without dish duty."

But Seth wanted things the way they'd always been. The day felt like a shirt that had grown scratchy. Where the heck was Selena? He checked his phone, feeling relieved when there were no texts from her. Every time the front door opened, he was in the hallway in seconds. But no Selena.

If it weren't for his latest discoveries, he would have been really bummed. The back door slammed open and a tiny hand tugged at his khaki pants. "Uncle Seth, when are we gonna have the Easter egg hunt?"

Seth smiled down at Darby, Malcolm's youngest. He'd been

given a liberal dose of his dad's red hair and freckles. "How about right now?"

The word spread like wildfire. Kids started screaming and McKenna joined the mayhem, handing out the buckets. Standing on his back deck, Seth counted to ten and yelled, "Go!" The five kids scattered and Seth was glad to see that Lisa, his only niece, was holding her own. While the boys spent most of their time shoving each other out of the way, she quietly plotted her course. In the midst of everything, Seth almost didn't notice the nudge at his elbow. But there was no mistaking Selena's scent. He turned.

Had Selena's smile always been this beautiful?

"Hey, babe." So automatic. For a second her eyes softened. A kiss would have come naturally too. But he hesitated. Where was Gary with all this?

Selena's eyes dimmed although the smile stayed put. "Happy Easter, Seth. I left my carrot cake in the kitchen."

"You didn't have to do that. You dropped off all that other stuff." One glance at her in that fluffy blue sweater and he couldn't recall exactly what she'd brought. The words escaped him. Her sweater hugged curves that would have made a roller coaster jealous. And her smile softened, like she knew it. "Thanks for coming."

"Told you I'd be here." A pretty pink flush added more color to her cheeks. He felt his family's eyes on them, especially McKenna's. The urge to push Selena's turtleneck aside and settle his lips on her warm neck made him crazy.

Somewhere along the way, he'd lost that right but he was taking it back, and soon.

Nipping her full lower lip, Selena swung her gaze out over the yard. "Looks like you've got a serious egg hunt going on here."

"Yep." He grabbed the railing to keep his hands busy.

Kids screamed while his brothers and their wives clapped.

"Come on, Lisa! *Andale!*" Selena hollered. "Don't let those boys win!" She pounded her fists on the railing like she was driving nails, the strikes reverberating up his arms. He'd always loved her competitive side, loved how she rooted for the underdog.

"Sometimes the boys win, Selena."

Fire sparked in her dark eyes. "Not if I can help it."

"Any double meaning here?"

"Take it however you like." She started backing away while frustration had a heyday in his chest. "Think I'll go talk to your mom."

The back storm door closed behind her just as all hell broke loose below. Pretty little Lisa had more eggs in her yellow basket than all the boys put together. That made them all chuckle, while the fathers tried to calm the boys down.

Just then McKenna clapped her hands. "Time to get this meal on the table." The women made a rush for the kitchen. Seemed that brunch was late and stomachs were rumbling. Seth was new to this host stuff and hadn't even been watching the time. He'd been too busy watching for Selena. McKenna started frying the hash browns while Amanda heated the sausage.

Relieved that they'd taken over, Seth turned back to the family room. He'd like to get Selena alone but for now he settled for studying her from the kitchen doorway. She perched on his mom's chair. Shadow was curled up in his mother's lap and the women seemed to be having a serious talk, making him uneasy.

"Good to see Selena here," Connor had joined him, Sean in his arms.

"Yeah. I guess."

"What's the deal with you two?"

"Wish I knew."

Seth smiled to see Sean trying to shove his own fingers into Connor's mouth. "What's your best guess?" his older brother asked.

The frustration of the last couple months knotted in his chest. "Just not doing something right, bro. Not doing the right stuff, not saying the right stuff. Guess I'm just a hot mess." Killed him to admit this, especially to Connor.

"You always were a late bloomer."

"Yeah. Right."

Connor's eyes followed his wife as she fooled with the serving table. "Once I got to know Amanda, I couldn't picture my life without her. That simple. Made me sick to even think about it. Like a puzzle piece that clicked in place, his brother's words fitted Seth's feelings. "You're right. Absolutely right. And Amanda? How did she know?"

Connor grinned. "I told her, egghead. I just told her."

But the words. What words did he use?

Seth was too embarrassed to ask. He almost whipped out the scrap of paper. But he was going to handle it himself.

"Connor!" Amanda waved him over. "Can you help me with this table?"

Appearing out of nowhere, Selena held out her arms. "Here, I'll take the baby."

With a smart-ass smile in Seth's direction, Connor handed over the baby and went to help his wife. Selena looked so natural cuddling Sean. He began to play with Selena's curls, his tiny fingers quickly tangled in them.

"*Ah, bambino. Qué haces, eh?*" Selena crooned. Extracting the baby's hand from her hair, she gave it a kiss. Smiling, Sean gurgled up at her.

"You're a natural with this, aren't you?" Seth was in awe of her.

"Am I?"

"Yeah, you definitely are."

Her eyes swung from the baby to him. "Seth, why didn't you ever tell me?"

"Tell you what?"

"About your problems in school? The teasing, the bullying?"

"That was nothing." Nothing that he wanted to relive. Instead, he studied Selena with the baby. They were alone huddled in a corner, while the kids outside screeched. But his own mother had outed him. Time to come clean. "Look, it's not easy to talk about it. Attention Deficit Disorder. Not exactly a manly quality."

"ADD?" Selena's face emptied. "Your mom was telling me about all the trouble you had on the playground in grade school."

Anger rolled over him in a hot wave. "Because of the ADD. She didn't mention that?"

Selena shook her head. Sean gave a little yelp and Selena shushed him. Connor and Amanda glanced over. "Everything's fine," Seth called out. Only it wasn't, not until Selena said something. His problem had seriously screwed up grade school. Time to explain it. "I was always in the principal's office for getting into fights on the playground. Couldn't sit still in class, so I found outlets. Those poor teachers."

"Your mom feels guilty. She wonders if she put too much pressure on you in school. So she was really talking about ADD? That's what got you into trouble all the time?" Her forehead puckered. This must be so hard for Selena to understand. She was never at a loss for words, doled them out like chocolate chips.

"That's crazy. It's nobody's fault."

"Is this why you don't want to go on with paramedic training?"

Thank God everyone was busy and no one paid any attention to them. "School wasn't easy. In class I never had the right answers or I stuttered, trying to get the words out. Of course kids teased me. You're so smart, Selena, but that wasn't the case with me. So I became the class clown. Made trouble for everybody." This was so damn humbling.

"Seth." How could her hand, so cool when she laid it on his arm, stoke a raging fire deep inside? But he couldn't pull away.

Selena looked like she wanted to say more but Sean was fussing.

"Sure, high school soured me even more." That's all he was going to say about it. "Besides, emergency medicine seemed like a good fit."

"But why didn't you tell me?"

But he didn't see any pity in her eyes. "What was there to say?"

"A lot. At least, I would have wanted to hear it."

Maybe. So he tried. "Here's the deal. In an ambulance, I'm boss. I can help people. That kind of pressure I can handle. I don't think, I just do. But personal stuff? Something else entirely." She was nodding her head and a tightness inside began to unwind.

"The words don't come easy and when they do, well, I have trouble getting them out, as you well know. It's like the words get stuck or trip over each other." Felt so good to say all this.

"Oh, *mi amor.* Who cares about that? I don't."

Sean started to wail and Selena jiggled the little guy and calmed him down, whispering in his ear. Seth had always wanted to learn Spanish but it would have meant another class.

His family had come inside and everyone wore a hungry look. For the first time in weeks, he wanted to eat. Connor and Amanda were fooling around at the eight-foot buffet table. Amazing that it didn't collapse under all that food. Every kind of salad he could imagine was spread out on the table. He'd noticed Logan sliding in with a couple of fancy bags from a downtown delicatessen near his expensive condo on Lake Shore Drive.

"Guess I should check on the kitchen." Leaving Selena with the baby, he wandered back into the kitchen, heavy with the smell of the egg casserole, sausage and hash browns. This had to be his favorite holiday meal.

"Brunch about ready?" he asked McKenna.

"Got the pot holders in place for the casserole? Logan will help you take the pans out." Steam rose from the pans and his sister's face had turned a pretty pink.

"Yep, I'll get him." But as he waved to Logan, his mind was back with Selena. How would she feel about what he'd just told her?

When the food was out and serving spoons in place, he began herding his family through the buffet line. Twenty chaotic minutes later, they were all seated at one of the three tables that crowded the dining room and spilled into the family room. Plates were piled high. His mother was beaming at him as if he'd done all this himself.

Seth felt pretty darn good, except for the fact that Selena was sitting down at the other end of the table. That part felt strange. Weird that she was here but so far away. But the day was far from over, at least for them.

His father started the family blessing and they all held hands. "We are a family today sharing our blessings, and for this we are very thankful." Maybe his dad had forgotten that Selena was here. But his mother looked pleased, nodding as his father rambled on, getting a little emotional. "And thank you for bringing our wife and mother back to health." He winked at Mom and she pressed one finger to her lips. She'd heard enough.

"Let's eat!" His dad nodded and silverware clinked.

At the other end of the table, Selena was talking to Joe, his younger brother. Unlike the Kirkpatricks in public service, Joe had studied architecture in Cincinnati. He'd scored a position with a firm in downtown Chicago. Looking at the two of them laughing, Seth realized with a start that they were about the same age.

Was that coffee burning in his stomach?

Joe glanced up and winked at him.

Seth had to make a move.

Chapter 15

Ay, caramba, every time Selena looked toward the end of the table, she met Seth's eyes. *Y Madre de Dios*, he looked so handsome in that pale blue shirt. Usually Seth wore T-shirts, which had never bothered her. In fact, she liked them. He filled them out in a good way. The oxford cloth shirt may have been for his mother's benefit but it struck a chord in her heart. He was one fine man. And his family was being so nice to her today, like they'd missed her. Connor had even caught her in the hallway and whispered, "Welcome back."

And then there was McKenna.

"How are things going?" her friend asked when they crossed paths at the bathroom door.

"Good. Seth has, well, shared some things you probably knew." Even she heard the hurt in her voice.

McKenna squeezed her arm. "It was his story to tell. Not mine."

"I understand." Things were falling into place.

Ten minutes later, she watched the family crowd onto the sofa. She sure hoped Seth had found the Selena Reminders she'd hidden late last Wednesday night. Glancing up, she caught his blush and relaxed.

When they were called to the table, she ended up next to Joe. She'd never spent much time with Seth's younger brother. But he was light-hearted fun today, which she needed. So much still had to be worked out. Her stomach felt jittery and she picked at her hash browns.

"If you don't eat those potatoes, I might have to eat them," Joe joked.

"Wouldn't want that to happen." But her throat closed when she thought of Seth on the playground. Her brothers would tell her that meeting adversity built character. "*La adversidad es la universidad.*" Isn't that what her father taught them? Never back away from a challenge. Obviously, Seth had worked through it.

Why hadn't he ever told her about his learning disability? She felt shut out. But didn't she have her own secret too? Time to take a chance. She pulled her attention back to the table.

"So, what project are you working on now?" she asked Joe.

"A commercial building downtown. Pretty exciting. I'm training as a project manager." His eyes sparkled, the way Seth's did when he talked about one of his life-saving runs. Joe dealt with buildings but Seth had lives in his hands. He may have had problems growing up, but he'd done an amazing job of moving forward in spite of them.

Amanda clinked a knife against her water glass. "Listen up, everyone. Harper couldn't be here today, but they're flying in soon for the couples' shower for McKenna and Logan."

"I'm in charge of the invitations," Jamie threw in. "If you know of anyone who should be on that list, give me a holler."

Amanda and McKenna began clearing the plates. Slices of carrot cake circled the table along with platters of bunny cookies. Mugs of coffee followed. Big Mike was usually in front of the TV by this time, turning on some game. Today he sat next to Reenie, trying to anticipate her every need. That man was so darn cute and his sons sure took after him.

Joe followed Selena's eyes. "I've never seen my father so worried."

"But she'll be fine."

"It'll take a while to convince Dad. He's just not himself."

The whole family probably felt that way, especially the sons. The Kirkpatricks were men to be reckoned with, but watching your mother struggle with a health issue? What did it do to a man when he saw that his father's whole world threatened to crumble when his wife got sick?

Every time she glanced down at Seth, her arms ached to soothe him. Selena began to clear empty dessert plates. Maureen reached for her as she passed. The woman still had a strong grip. Before Selena knew it, she was pulled into the seat vacated by McKenna. "Selena, tell me about your visit to Savannah. We never did get to talk about that."

Selena launched into a description of her time with Harper. She knew Maureen missed her youngest daughter. "Cameron's a fine man. He'll make a good husband for Harper."

"Glad to hear you say that, Selena. Mike and I feel the same way. Cameron will be a great addition to the family." Then she stopped and nipped her lip. "Sorry, sweetheart, I didn't mean that you…"

Selena patted Reenie's hand. "Not to worry. I know what you mean. Guess it's my turn to help in the kitchen." Ready to jump out of her skin, Selena took the stack of plates out to the sink. Plunging her hands into the soapy water, Selena scrubbed pans in spite of McKenna's protests. "I got this, McKenna. Why don't you help Amanda fill the dishwasher?" The men had been banished to the family room where the TV blared.

The day was ending and she should leave. But so much filled her heart. She just couldn't leave Seth's house. Not yet.

~.~

The women had pushed Seth out of the kitchen and that was okay, except he hated to leave Selena. His brothers and dad had the TV blaring and the kids were screaming outside. Needing a break, Seth headed down to his man cave.

He was a man on a mission.

Grabbing some empty boxes on his way through the game room, he pressed against a section of the back paneling. A door swung open. There was a time when he thought that was cool. Not anymore. In fact, he felt embarrassed. Lining his boxes up on the top shelf, he went to work.

Behind him, the panel clicked open again and he turned, ready to chop someone's head off for invading his space.

"What are you doing down here?" Connor glanced around. Seth's oldest brother always did everything right, although he'd shown his human side during the years when he and Amanda tried so hard to have a baby. But he didn't want Connor to see what he was doing.

"Just cleaning up." The framed pictures felt heavy in his hands. Quickly, Seth buried them in a box.

With the attitude of a fireman who'd be chief one day, Connor moved toward the shelving and picked up a picture. "What you got here?"

Seth ground his molars. "Senior Prom."

"Dude. That was so long ago." The look on his brother's face twisted in Seth's gut.

"Fine times, bro."

But Connor was shaking his head. Oh, the baseball and basketball trophies were fine but when he got to the pictures of girls Seth used to date? Different story. "What is this, your trophy case?"

"Of course not." More pictures clattered into the box. He never paid much attention to these shelves anymore. In fact, he rarely came down here. The man cave had served a purpose when he built it. Now? For football and Nascar Sundays, his family room was the place to be. His brother was right. This had been his trophy room in more ways than one. Time to shut it down.

Connor picked up another photo. "Good grief, Seth. Is this Mercy McCray? With braces?"

Seth's lips felt numb. "Sophomore year homecoming."

"Pathetic."

The word tunneled into his gut. "You know what? You're right." Mercy and sophomore year went into the box.

"Is this why Selena dumped you?"

"She didn't dump me... well, yeah, I guess she did. But she never saw this." *Thank God.*

Wearing a look that his kids would probably learn to dread, Connor stood back. "You're lucky, man. You'd never hear the end of it. Amanda would have killed me for keeping pictures of girls I dated."

"Yeah. Probably. I just never thought of it that way." Amanda was sweet and laid back compared to Selena, who had more of a scorched earth policy when she got mad.

His brother regarded him, a small smile dancing across his lips. "I never realized you were so sentimental."

"I'm not."

"Oh yes you are." Connor was holding a shot of Seth with Selena at a St. Patrick's Day party. Grabbing it from his brother's hands, Seth set it back on the shelf. Shamrocks painted on both cheeks, she'd never looked more beautiful. They'd had a great time that night.

"Good thing you're getting rid of all this." Connor peered over the edge of the box. "This is the past, man. You have to move on."

Seth gave a resigned sigh. "I realize that, Connor."

"You sign up for the paramedic course yet?"

His eyes snagged on a shot of him with Selena at Navy Pier. The last time he'd seen this picture, it was in Selena's bedroom. His pulse pounded in his ears. She'd been down here? He was toast.

"Seth?" Connor's voice brought him back "What about the paramedic training?"

He left the photo sitting right where it was. "I'll get to the course, so stay off my case."

"You're going to be thirty-one this year."

"Thank you for reminding me." Cold sweat dampening his forehead, Seth slumped back into the chair. Connor took the old beat-up sofa across from him.

"I'm just saying, it's time to shape up your life, Seth. You want to be single all your life? Fine. You want to be an EMT instead of advancing up the ranks and becoming a paramedic, fine. But I don't think that's true."

"Maybe we don't want the same things, okay?"

Connor looked like Seth had just slugged him. "Why? Am I that bad?"

Seth snorted. "No, you're that good. Good at everything. And I know it sounds weird but Dad always liked you best…"

"That is not true—"

What? Was Connor blind? "It *is* true. So I wanted to be different than you." He glanced over at his empty shelves. "Because I couldn't be better."

"Hey, I was never big with the ladies, Seth. Not like you. And Mom always liked you best."

"Get out of here."

They both roared and Seth was glad they were in the basement.

Besides cleaning up down here, he wanted to practice what he was going to say. Selena was not leaving today without hearing it, especially after his latest findings. He was on firm footing, ready to run his next play.

Chapter 16

No one was leaving the family party and Selena needed time alone with Seth before she took off. He'd disappeared downstairs and she knew what he'd find there, if he noticed the latest addition to his photo collection.

"Anyone know where Connor is?" Amanda stood in the middle of the kitchen, Sean in her arms. "Everyone is waiting to say good-bye."

"Probably downstairs with Seth, Amanda." Catching the baby's waving hand, Selena kissed it. So very soft.

"Well I'm not going down there." Amanda looked ticked off. Didn't she realize she had everything?

Big Mike was leaving with Reenie and they brushed behind her.

"So good to see you, dear." Reenie gave Selena a kiss on the cheek. "Stop by now, you hear?"

"Sure." And she hoped she'd have great news the next time she saw her. "You take care now, Reenie, okay?"

Big Mike helped his wife with her coat and then steered her toward the door. "Tell the boys we said good-bye. They must be downstairs and I have to get their mom home. See you, Selena."

"We're heading out too!" Malcolm and Dana were right behind them, kids in tow. Joe had left earlier. He had a big date, or so

Amanda had told Selena.

Should she go downstairs to find Seth and Connor? Amanda looked so tired. She'd plopped into a chair with the baby and Selena pushed a hassock under her swollen ankles.

Mark and Jamie were next out the door, James and Randy squabbling over whose plastic bunny was bigger.

A crack of thunder announced the storm. The sky opened and rain poured down in gray sheets, wind rattling against the windows. From the family room window, she couldn't even see the garage.

Connor and Seth suddenly appeared. "Sorry, honey. Guy talk." Connor kissed Amanda on the cheek and took his son so his wife could pull on her coat.

Selena felt strange standing there. "Maybe I'll hit the road too, Seth. Thank you... for everything."

"Stay for a minute, okay?"

Relief rippled through her. "Sure."

Seth's eyes darted around. "Anyone seen Shadow?"

Selena set her purse down. "No, not lately."

"The kids had the cat." Amanda peered into the empty box Seth had brought. "But I haven't seen her for a while."

"Tell you the truth, everyone's been in and out all day." Connor shifted the whimpering baby in his arms. "You think she'd go outside if she had a chance?"

"Maybe. She's a wild cat." Worry furrowed Seth's brow. Another burst of lightning was followed by thunder that sounded like boulders shifting under the house. Wherever Shadow was, she must be terrified.

The baby cried harder. "Connor and Amanda, go ahead and leave," Seth told them. "I'm sure Shadow's around here somewhere. I'll find her."

"I'll help you look," Selena offered. The rain was coming down hard and Shadow was such a little thing.

"I'll bring the car around," Connor told Amanda, handing Sean to his wife and disappearing out the door.

Selena turned to Seth. "Why don't you take the second floor and I'll check the family room and the closets?"

Leaving Amanda in the front hall with Sean, Selena started searching the family room and living room. She looked under the sofas, checked behind doors and opened every closet door, even the cabinets under the kitchen counters. No little gray kitty.

Meanwhile, Connor pulled up and came in for Amanda. "Found the cat yet?"

"No." Selena shook her head. "She might be upstairs and Seth is checking."

The front door was closing behind Connor and Amanda when Seth came down the steps empty-handed.

"Nothing?"

He shook his head. "No. Maybe she's downstairs. Connor and I were down there and the door was open. She's so darn curious."

"I'm right behind you."

Seth flicked on the lights and down they went, calling the cat as they looked. But no small bunch of fur bounded out from the under the furniture, no long tail swished across their legs. She didn't seem to be anywhere. Passing the pool table and the ice hockey game, Seth pushed a panel. The wall opened. "My man cave. But then you know about this."

"I do. Very James Bond." Did he think this was a secret?

Ruddy complexion deepening, Seth shrugged. "Stupid is more like it. Hardly ever use it anymore. But Connor and I had the door open. Shadow? You here, girl?" They started to search the room that smelled closed up and empty.

While he checked in some boxes and under the furniture, Selena was drawn to the framed photos on the black shelving, especially the shot of them. Her contribution to Seth's collection. She could almost feel the sun, hear the gulls and smell the water.

She could almost feel the love. "Seth?"

Coming closer, he followed her eyes. "I've still got hope, Selena. You have to know that."

Hope? Warmth unfurled in her chest like a spring flower.

But right now they had to find Shadow.

"Got some umbrellas? Let's look outside."

They tromped back up the stairs. "Why don't you stay in the house? It's miserable out there." Seth rummaged through the back closet and pulled out his Chicago Bears umbrella.

"No way." She grabbed another one from a hook on the back of the door. "This is a two-person job."

"Let me have that small one." He hesitated, always the gentleman. Water fell from the overhang in a liquid gray sheet.

"Team effort." Pulling the back door open, Selena stepped out and snapped the umbrella open. "Come on."

While thunder rumbled, they checked under all the bushes

surrounding the house. "Shadow? Shadow!" The wind whipped her umbrella inside out and she tossed it aside. Her silver jacket quickly became a wet weight on her shoulders.

"Why don't you go inside, Selena? You're soaked."

"I'm not going to leave you out here. Let's try the neighbors. Canvas a wider area."

The light was failing and Selena's stomach tightened. Poor little Shadow. *Pobrecita.* Wherever she was, she must be scared to death. What if they couldn't find the kitten before dark? The neighbors' outside lights were coming on. Together they rang doorbells and asked neighbors to keep an eye out for the small gray cat. But with every house, Seth looked more discouraged. The rain never let up.

"Let's get some warm coffee." Selena's teeth were chattering and that was probably the only reason Seth agreed to go inside for a bit.

While the coffee brewed, she threw their wet jackets in the dryer. Together they hunched at the counter, sipping coffee in an uncomfortable silence.

"Thanks for staying to help me, Selena."

"Not a problem." He looked almost as miserable as she felt. "Do you think she wandered off? Maybe scared by all the noise?"

"Could be. I don't know much about cats. Maybe I'm too stupid to own one." When he shook his head in frustration, droplets hit the counter.

"Stop that. You rescued Shadow. From what you said, she might not have made it through that cold night. You're the kind of guy who, well, saves people... or animals." Was she making sense?

"That's sweet, Selena. But I think I'm the kind of guy who needs rescuing himself."

Such a plea. She cupped his face with one hand. "Don't be so hard on yourself, *cariño.*"

With a crooked smile, he brushed her chin with his thumb. "Well, I do try."

"*Sí, de veras.* You sure do."

His eyes swam with love. She felt it, as surely as the rain that thundered outside. Wasn't that enough? His touch on her skin awakened every nerve in her body. Seth was so close. She could feel the warmth of his breath and she shivered.

"You still cold? I'll get a blanket."

He jumped up and she felt the chill.

Seth was the warmth of her life. Always would be.

"No, not really..."

He brought a throw from the sofa anyway and wrapped it around her shoulders. "So, where's Gary today? Did he leave you to fend for yourself?" The smile had disappeared.

"We're not seeing each other anymore," she said softly. "You should know that after finding my toothbrush. Besides, we were just friends."

"Really? Friends?" Seth's eyes narrowed like he didn't believe her. "What man could be just friends with you?"

"You think I'm that irresistible?"

"I *know* so." Seth's brown eyes warmed and he exhaled. "Well, that's news."

"Good news?"

"That depends." An eyebrow lifted. No man could ever look as innocent yet badass as Seth Kirkpatrick. "Come here, Selena." He tugged her onto his lap.

His kiss began with her lips but the heat shot through her body. Dropping the blanket and sinking into him, she couldn't get enough. Drank him in with her kisses. She wanted long hearty draughts that filled her, left her satisfied.

"Oh, Selena, baby." Tightening his embrace, Seth rocked her. She could almost feel the wheels turning in his head. "I need to tell you. I-I love you. God, how I m-missed you. I missed you so bad."

Her head jerked back. "What did you just say?"

"I missed you?"

She circled the air with a finger. "No, the first part."

"I love you?"

"*Sí, sí. Te amo.*" She hugged his words to her heart.

He blushed. "Is it that simple?" And he opened his lips as if to say more. The wrinkle in his forehead told her he was searching.

Reaching out she stroked his cheek, stubble rasping against her fingers. "Why are you so lost?"

He caught her hand and kissed it. Then he lifted troubled eyes. "I am, babe. Or I was. You're the only one who can rescue me. Seriously."

"I think you know how to rescue yourself."

"Apparently not. I don't know where I'm going without you."

"But you don't have to be without me." With a soft laugh, she squeezed his hand. Time to level with him. "You know, I should have guessed about the ADD. But you're a proud man. I don't know if I would have brought it up. Seth, I haven't been totally honest with you either. You know when I talked about my folks and how they worked a farm?"

"Yeah, right. Up in Michigan."

"Well, there wasn't just one farm, there were many. We were migrant workers. You people might call us drifters or illegals, but we went where the work was to make a living."

Jaw shifting, he seemed to be taking in her words. "Sounds like a hard life. Why didn't you tell me?"

She looked down at their linked hands. "Guess I was embarrassed, Seth. I'm about as far from an Oak Park girl as I can be. Every thing I owned was in my pink Barbie doll backpack. Got it at Goodwill and used it until I was fourteen."

"Nothing to be ashamed of," he said, matter-of-fact as always.

"Guess I was. I'll never be a homecoming queen or a cheerleader. We were never in one place long enough to make friends."

His kiss on her forehead felt like total acceptance. "No wonder you're so special, Selena. I have nothing but respect for you." His voice held wonder. What a guy. The tight knot in her chest eased as the shame faded.

"Really, as in put me on a pedestal?"

A naughty chuckle rumbled in his throat. "No, as in, put you in my bed."

Ah hah. She took a deep breath. The surge of desire awakened every nerve in its path. She flicked a thumb over his calluses and traced some scratches with a finger. "You've been working."

"The scratches are from Shadow." Such sadness in his face.

"She still has her claws?"

He nodded. "I didn't have the heart."

Sliding off his lap, Selena headed for the laundry room.

"Where you going?"

"To get our jackets and check out the trees."

The stool crashed to the floor when he leapt up. "I'm right behind you."

Although the rain had eased, they were soaked again by the time they found Shadow huddled high in a tree. "I'm calling a vet in the morning about those claws," Seth grumbled, dragging a ladder from his garage.

But they were both so relieved. The poor little thing was mewling pathetically once Seth got to her. She must have climbed up so high and then didn't know how to get down. Hair plastered to her body, she looked no bigger than a branch. Snuggling her inside his jacket, Seth made his way back down. Once they got her inside, it took awhile to dry the kitten off with a towel and the hair dryer.

"Now where were we?" Seth asked later when they were cuddled on the couch together. Shadow snoozed right next to them, exhausted by her adventure.

"You were a sorry mess."

Gently taking her knees, Seth lifted them onto his lap, careful not to disturb the cat. "I am, babe."

"*Claro.* You can say that again. Your mom helped me understand part of it. You couldn't tell me?" A muscle twitched in his jaw, and she chuckled, slowly running a finger over the strong line of the bone. "What's wrong? What's hurting?"

"My pride." His crooked smile made him look so darned cute. "It's hard to admit that some things come slowly. I'm not quick like Connor...or Joe. Never have been."

"You don't have to be, Seth. You're a good man, a strong man in every way that matters. At least to me. Besides, some women like it slower." She pulled the last words out like warm taffy, loving the way his expression heated.

In a lot of ways, Seth was a quick learner.

In all the ways that mattered. But it took her a while to get that.

The light in his eyes told her he totally understood. "Have I messed things up by not speaking up?" His uncertainty was endearing.

"Maybe. Maybe not." She liked to toy with him.

"I have a habit of putting my foot in my mouth."

Giggles choked her at the helpless look in his eyes and she swallowed them. Selena knew from her brothers that laughing would be the worst thing she could do right now. So where could she go? His dark eyes pleaded with her.

"Try me," Selena whispered. "Just try me. Tell me and take your time."

A muscle twitched in his neck. His lips worked. "I love you, Selena. I can't get any f-fancier than that. I'll make a fool of myself. When my sentences get longer they turn into f-fishing tackle, dragging me down."

She'd waited so long and she wanted to hear these words again and again. "Can we go back to the first part? The love part? Don't think I got all of it earlier."

His teasing grin melted her heart. "Of course I love you. Probably have since I first saw you. Love your spirit... your kindness... your passion."

He put each word out there like a present.

"Even though you broke all my dishes. Hey... what's this? Are you crying? Babe, I'm kidding."

"No, I'm laughing. Will you ever get over those broken plates?" She wiped her eyes.

"Hell, no." Now he was laughing too. "They were expensive, right? I hate the fact that you had to buy them again."

"My mother would be horrified. But what's a few dishes when a woman has to make a point? Got your attention, right?"

His hold on her tightened until they felt like one. "You always have my attention."

Where was a tissue when you needed it? He frowned at the tear he lifted from her cheek with a finger. "No, no tears, babe." His lips angled over hers. The kiss left her breathless. "You're not saying anything," he murmured. "So will you... ?"

"You're not letting me."

"And the answer?"

"What was the question?"

He sucked in a breath. She was being terrible, making him go through all this. But she was really enjoying it.

"Will you, Selena Ruiz, marry me?"

Talk about getting right to the point. "When you decided to put

it out there, it's, well, all out there. Yes, you crazy, sweet man. Yes."
She thought her heart would pulse right out of her chest. "But we
say nothing until after McKenna's wedding, *claro?*"

His eyes clouded. "Why?"

"Because it will be too much for your mother. She will get
crazy. Harper got engaged in February and now us? *Mi amor,* trust
me. One engagement at a time. Yes, we are back together but no
ring." She wiggled her bare left hand. "Not for a while. A little
while."

"You're probably right. Now, no more talking," he growled,
pushing her back on the sofa. "I might say the wrong thing and
mess up again."

"Never. You will never mess this up because I love you. You
are my big, bad *hombre y te amo.*"

Some things didn't need translating.

Bending, he unzipped one of her boots so slowly she could hear
every click. Sexier than all get out. Eyes flashing, he tugged it off.
She curled her toes. "Now the other one."

Pressing one hand to her chest, she held her breath, held it so
she could hear every click of the other zipper. Once he'd taken care
of that, he went for her mini skirt, hands skimming the leather,
showing her how much he cared.

"I've missed you so much," she whispered in his ear, before
nipping his ear lobe so hard he yelped.

"And to think I have this to come home to for the rest of my
life."

"Yes, if you take your classes, if you..."

What was she saying? She was almost glad when he touched one finger to her lips. "What's this? Setting conditions?"

Shame curdled her new-found confidence. "You do what you want." The words came hard because she wanted so much *for* him. But this all had to be his choice.

His eyes softened. "Trust me, okay? I do want more. You are my inspiration, Selena, you really are. With you I can do more, be more. I was lost without you."

"Oh, Seth." While he tended to her skirt zipper, she worked on the tiny buttons of his shirt.

"You? You would never be lost." " He whisked off her sweater but she wasn't cold. Spring had finally come and raging heat sizzled in her veins.

"But I was. Without you? Lost." When Seth bent his head to nuzzle her neck and work lower, Selena wriggled with contentment. "You're the man I can't walk away from." Pulling the tails of his shirt out of his jeans, she yanked until the last two buttons loosened.

He pulled her upright. "How about a hot shower?"

"Sounds good."

Now dry, Shadow followed them upstairs, halting with disapproval when clothes went flying. When they disappeared into the bathroom, Shadow continued into the bedroom. She'd probably had enough water for one day.

Over the next half hour, they discovered that the shelf in his shower had been a good addition. Making up for lost time might take a while.

Cuddling in his bed later felt so right. When Seth lowered his eyelids, those ridiculously long lashes fanned over his cheeks.

"Hope our daughters have your eyelashes." They prickled when she ran a finger lightly over the tips.

"I hope they have your passion." Pulling back, he appeared to think about that. "No, wait a minute. I would be seriously outnumbered. Maybe we can compromise?"

"Always a good thing."

"And let's remember, dishes are for eating."

Nodding slowly, she trailed a hand down his six-pack. "And words are for communicating."

The groan came low in his throat. "You do a pretty good job with your hands, babe. Makes it hard... to... think." She laughed when he flipped her over, scaring the cat right off the bed. In the next hour, Seth proved that he was a man of action not words, a point Selena wanted to always remember.

Chapter 17

The Christo de Sangre mountains rose in jagged purple peaks against the setting sun. Arm in arm, Seth and Selena strolled up Canyon Road. They'd come to Santa Fe for McKenna's wedding but the last two days had been an amazing vacation. Tomorrow was the wedding ceremony and the dinner tonight at El Farol offered a special treat with tapas and flamenco dancing. But best of all, she was here with Seth. Selena snuggled closer and felt him kiss the top of her head.

"We might have to come back and visit your brother some time. So much to take in." Seth looked around at the adobe galleries lining the narrow street. Puffs of dust kicked up when a car ventured slowly past them on the narrow one-way road.

"If we come back, Rafael and Ana would want us to stay with them," Selena managed with a straight face, knowing what Seth's response would be. "They have a spare room."

Horror rippled over his face. "Are you kidding? And miss the hot tub at the inn? No way."

"Thought you'd see it that way. The hot tub is one thing. That breakfast buffet?" She patted her hips. "I'm already putting on weight."

"You look perfect," he murmured. "All this walking should

keep both of us in shape. Especially this hill."

"Good for our thighs." Flanked with shops and art galleries, Canyon Road went for blocks, all on an upward angle.

"Trust me, *amor*. No work needed on any part of your legs."

"Maybe I wasn't talking about mine."

The rumble of laughter in Seth's chest made her smile. "Selena Ruiz, soon to be Selena Kirkpatrick, you are a tease."

Smiling up at him, Selena basked in his love. After the tension of the past three months, this certainty felt more soothing than the hot tub last night.

Seth's phone pinged. Checking the screen, he smiled. "Good news from Amanda. Sean rolled over for the first time. Guess he was trying to keep his eyes on Shadow."

"A win-win, right? Good thing we had Shadow declawed. Amanda was so good to take care of the kitten."

Slipping the phone back in his pocket, Seth nodded. "I have a feeling Sean and Shadow might turn out to be buddies. Connor stopped over last Saturday with Sean to watch part of the game. I couldn't believe it when Shadow dragged her favorite stuffed mouse over to the baby in his bouncy seat."

"I love the way your brother lets Amanda have her girl time on the weekend."

"So, you're hoping that's a family trait, right?"

She squeezed his waist. "You've always been a smart man."

He lifted a brow, like he didn't believe it. But her husband-to-be was beaming. Then his expression shifted. Changing course, Seth detoured down a side street and backed her up against a long adobe wall. She welcomed every firm angle of his body. "When it comes to you, I hope I always am. Tell me if you're not hearing what you need to hear, *mi amor*." He nibbled on her neck and she shivered in the dry heat.

"So you'll be my 'yes' man?" she teased, twitching her hips.

Closing his eyes, Seth seemed to consider that thought. Or was he just enjoying her bump and grind? With a low shudder, he shook his head. "Not exactly and you know it." His hands tightened on her hips. She gave another sassy swish and he groaned.

The warm adobe heated her back when Seth did his best to make her wish they weren't in a public place. Good thing the side street was empty. Weathered strings of red peppers swayed in the doorway next to them. Selena jumped when one brushed her shoulder. She nipped his ear lobe. "Guess we should remember where we are."

Seth backed off but not much. "Most of the tourists are back at their hotels, getting ready for dinner. Besides, Santa Fe is so romantic. A little PDA wouldn't shock anyone."

"Your family will be waiting for us." They had just come from the Loretto Chapel and were headed to the rehearsal dinner. Big Mike and Connor both had rented SUVs and had driven some of the family up the road to the restaurant. Since Mallory and Amy had arrived at the Albuquerque airport at the same time as Vanessa and Alex, they were sharing a vehicle. But Seth and Selena preferred to walk. The night felt so soft and she wanted every second possible with her man.

With a glance toward the road, Seth grinned. "My family can wait. The Kirkpatricks are all about taking things slow." He lowered his head, kissing her as if he could not get enough. She sighed with contentment, drinking in the sweet scent of wisteria winding over the ledge above.

"Hungry?" he asked, pulling away.

"Yep." She brushed her lips against his one more time. "But not for food."

Cupping her cheeks in his palms, Seth lowered his forehead to hers. "Did I ever tell you how much I love you? How I can't wait to marry you?"

That twirly feeling in her chest? Pure happiness. "Never get tired of hearing it." Ever since Easter, Seth had made sure that she knew how he felt—not easy for this guy.

I can't know unless you tell me had become their mantra.

"Come on. According to the map, the restaurant's right ahead." Taking her hand, he steered her back onto Canyon Road.

She sighed. Some secrets were so hard to keep.

Although Seth's family knew they were back together, they seemed to sense things had changed between them. Or was Selena just imagining things? They'd agreed that they would wait until after the wedding to announce their engagement. "Every bride wants to be the center of attention," she had reasoned with Seth and he agreed that McKenna deserved her moment with Logan.

Besides, the Kirkpatricks already had another engagement to celebrate. Everyone had been so excited to see Harper's engagement ring when Cameron and Harper arrived from the airport yesterday. They'd all celebrated at the afternoon wine and cheese get-together in the lounge of the inn. It made Selena so happy to think she'd been with Harper and Cameron for that proposal last February. She treated the family to every last detail she could recall, especially for Reenie's benefit. How far Selena had come since her visit to Savannah when she'd felt so broken. And Harper had been such a help. Although she may be the spitfire of the family, her experiences with Cameron had made her into a wise woman.

"Selena, I'm so happy for you," Harper had whispered to her when they ran into each other at breakfast that morning. "Looks like things are going well with Seth."

"Thanks for all your advice. Maybe you were my lucky charm."

Bella was with Connie back in Savannah, giving Harper some much needed time alone with Cameron in Santa Fe. How Selena wanted to tell Harper that Seth had proposed. But this was a secret worth keeping for a while.

Last night, Seth and Selena had taken plastic glasses of sangria down to one of the inn's hot tubs. Gazing up at the azure sky of New Mexico, she'd wondered if they might want to be married here. The city cast such a magic spell.

But no need to hurry anything.

The decision had been a long time coming. She wanted to savor it.

"I enjoyed meeting your brother Rafael and Ana today." Seth pulled her attention back. Rafael and his wife had met them for lunch at the old fashioned diner on the plaza.

"He told me I was one lucky girl. I had to set him straight, of course."

"Your brother adores you. I'm looking forward to spending more time with your family."

"I told my parents we would visit Kalamazoo again this summer. My mother sounded suspicious. Maybe we can go up there after we announce our engagement to your family."

"What? You never took Gary there?"

Selena socked Seth playfully. "I'll probably never hear the end of this, right?"

"Afraid so." Seth gave her a wry grin.

Gary and Mindy were back together and Selena might never know the rest of that story. What a different experience to commiserate with a man, but helpful to get a masculine perspective on a breakup. Whenever she saw her former pretend boyfriend in the hall at work, he looked content. She shared that feeling.

Seth's steps slowed. "Wait a minute. You're talking about telling your parents this summer? I was thinking we'd be married this summer."

Whoa. That brought Selena up sharp. "Really? That fast?"

"Sure. I thought maybe we'd have the ceremony after my paramedic sessions were over."

"This is news. You're scheduled for classes? That's terrific."

He puffed out his chest. "Am I a changed man or what? I wanted to surprise you."

Selena's mind clicked ahead. "I'm going to Guatemala in July on my mission trip."

"Yes, of course I remember. But what about August?"

Who was this man? "You know, I have to get used to this new Seth, the guy who makes plans."

Throwing back his head, he laughed. The setting sun sculpted the handsome planes of his face. She'd never seen him so happy. Had love really done this to him?

Some of the shops were still open. One window displayed elegant silver jewelry set with opals and her steps slowed. "What beautiful pieces. Look at the stones."

"We've got time. Come on." A tiny bell rang when Seth opened the door.

Inside, the narrow shop was lined with glass cases. An opal necklace caught Selena's eye. The stone seemed to capture the unusual blue of the Santa Fe sky.

"Could we see that?" Seth motioned to the clerk, who was happy to oblige.

Lifting her hair, Selena gazed into the viewing mirror while Seth fastened the delicate chain around her neck.

"Like it?" He caught her eye in the reflection.

"It's beautiful." She trailed her fingers over the stone, wondering how expensive it was.

"Then we'll take it."

She touched his arm as the clerk whisked the necklace away. "Oh, Seth. Isn't it too much?"

"I've been putting in overtime. Consider it your engagement necklace, until we choose the right ring."

"Can I wear it now?"

"Absolutely."

As they continued their walk up Canyon Road, Selena brushed the necklace with her left hand. Sometimes she felt as if she were living a dream. They'd come full circle over the past three months. Didn't every couple follow their own course? She was so grateful that for them, the journey would have a happy ending.

At last they'd reached the wide log porch of El Farol and climbed the steps. She couldn't wait to see everyone. They'd been so scattered all day, all of them eager to take in as much as they could during this short visit. A waiter led them to a room in the back where the Kirkpatrick family and close friends waited. Small candles cast a warm glow on the long tables that bracketed a dance floor. Tiny white lights looped from the ceiling, adding to the magic and mystery.

"So romantic," Selena whispered, happy to be a part of the Kirkpatrick family again.

"About time you two got here." Big Mike waved to them from the far side of the dance floor.

"Front row seats," Seth said, his hand on Selena's back as they moved toward the group. "Watch your step now."

Reenie was seated between her husband and Cecile, Logan's grandmother. The two older women had their heads together. What a relief that Reenie's recovery was going so well. Amy and Vanessa were deep in conversation with Harper. Everyone seemed to be catching up.

"Have a good day?" McKenna asked from the foot of the long table, once Seth and Selena were seated.

"Fabulous but we may need a return trip."

"That can probably be arranged." McKenna looked so happy, Logan's arm around her. Such a perfect pair. Beaming, McKenna looked as if she might be thinking the same thing about Seth and Selena.

Wine was served and Connor proposed a toast to the bride and groom. "May your love and devotion grow with every year together." Glasses clinked and Logan's grandmother dabbed at her eyes. Selena wondered what the toast would be at their own dinner. Summer? Really? In more ways than one, Seth took her breath away.

The waitress arrived and they chose their tapas. It felt different for the family not to have the children with them, different but kind of nice. Conversation flowed and they all took their time, sampling and sharing. No one had to break away to monitor the children. The room was partially open on the sides and the soothing night air wafted into the room. Back in Chicago, spring still struggled to get a foothold so the milder weather in Santa Fe sure felt good.

In a sudden change of mood, a man in full Spanish costume leapt onto the stage. Strumming his guitar with agile fingers, he tilted his gilt-edged black sombrero against the spotlight trained on the center of the stage. Conversation halted when the flamenco dancers took the floor, stomping, clapping and wailing of heartbreak and honor. The performance resonated in her heart but not as strongly as Seth's smile in the darkness.

Afterwards, the group lingered over coffee. Seth's arm around the back of her chair, Selena savored the contentment.

"What a pretty necklace," Harper commented when she circled the table. "Is that an opal?"

"Gift from your brother." Catching Seth's eye, Selena smiled.

Harper's eyes narrowed. "And why do I think this gorgeous piece of jewelry is something more than just a necklace?"

Lifting her brows, Selena said nothing more. Thank goodness Harper didn't press her.

After dinner, Seth and Selena strolled back toward the hotel, while the others piled into the SUVs. Night had fallen softly. It felt almost eerie to pass the darkened storefronts. When they reached the deep garden of a metal sculptor, his creations whirred gently in the breeze.

"Should we go to the hot tub tonight?" she asked when they reached the bottom of the road and turned right toward Alameda and the inn.

"I overheard Logan talking to McKenna about the hot tub. Four is definitely a crowd. Think I have a different idea. "

"But aren't there two tubs in two different locations?"

"Not taking any chances. We need some private time. I picked up some massage oils today while you were trying on clothes."

~~

As the harpist played in the Loretto Chapel the following morning, Selena waited her turn in the back of the church with McKenna. The small, intimate chapel seemed so perfect for the service. In the front sat Reenie, along with Grandma Cecile. No groom's or bride's side for this group. Some close friends were scattered through the chapel, all eyes on the front where the men were lined up, handsome in black tuxedoes.

Vanessa had gone first, stunning with her midnight hair contrasting with the deep pink gown. Then came Amy with her sweet smile, Mallory's eyes following her every step. Was he remembering their wedding on the cruise ship docked outside Venice? Next to him in the third pew sat Cameron, who snapped shots as Harper started down the aisle. No doubt Bella was eager to see wedding photos. Of course, a photographer was at the front to document the entire service.

"See you at the altar, girlfriend." Selena hugged McKenna, whose fiery hair tumbled past her shoulders in long curls.

"Are you next?" McKenna whispered. "Something sure seems different about you two."

Selena hoped her expression didn't give her away. "I think Harper might beat me to the altar." She had to throw McKenna off the trail or there would be no end to the questions.

"Ah, hah. Your turn to walk down the aisle. In this wedding party, I mean." McKenna's attention turned toward the front where Logan waited.

Selena's eyes found Seth. He was the only one who mattered as she traversed the short aisle. Heads already were craning toward the back, all attention on the bride.

Her bouquet quivering in her hands, Selena joined the ladies and turned. The harpist paused and began Pachelbel's canon in D.

McKenna was a sight to behold as she came down the aisle on Big Mike's arm. Delicately understated, her beaded gown cupped her figure in a shaped bell that trailed into a short train. Usually not a woman who fussed, today McKenna was a fashion statement. A puff of meringue, her veil fell past her skirt, held in place on her red curls with white hyacinths and stephanotis that filled the gothic arches of the chapel with sweetness.

Selena couldn't help the tears in her eyes, and Seth shot her a concerned look as his sister took Logan's arm and they all turned. "Love you," he mouthed. She smiled back and the service began.

At the dinner later, McKenna did the traditional bouquet toss. Selena was amazed to catch it instead of Harper. It almost seemed as if McKenna had thrown the flowers straight to her in the small semi-circle of single women. When it came time for the man's boutonniere, Selena half expected Seth to duck out as he had in at past weddings.

Today Seth was full of surprises. This time, he stepped right up, hands waving in the air, like he was signaling to the quarterback. When Seth leapt to snatch the flower Logan tossed, Harper gave Selena a pointed glance. Dropping her eyes, Selena wasn't saying anything. Seth swaggered back to the table, the hyacinth sprig pinned proudly in his lapel.

Family members gave each other pleased smiles.

Sometimes words weren't needed.

Epilogue

Three Months Later

Wedding bells pealed, filling St. Edmund Church and Selena's heart with joy. Her mother fussed with the train of Selena's wedding gown and turned to her younger sister. Poor Sofia was Selena's maid of honor. In their mother's eyes, this responsibility ranked close to Homeland Security. "Now, Sofia. *Ten cuido. Es importante que todo es perfecto.*"

"*Sí, mama.*" Sofia caught Selena's eyes and smiled. "Everything will be perfect."

"Don't worry. You'll have your turn," Selena whispered.

"All set?" McKenna poked her head in from the bridesmaids' dressing room next door. Her mouth fell open when Selena turned from the long mirror.

"Oh, my. Who else could look smoking hot and sexy on her wedding day? Has Seth seen this?"

Smoothing one hand over the deep flamenco ruffles that flared onto the floor, Selena shook her head. She couldn't wait to see Seth's expression. He'd be sorry the dress didn't cut up in the front, like flamenco dancers. She'd had the dressmaker make some necessary modifications. After all, they were in a church.

"We're going to need smelling salts for Seth." McKenna fanned herself with one hand.

"Blame it on your Santa Fe wedding, McKenna." Mimicking the dancers, she kicked one foot out under the train and turned. Selena had practiced the tricky maneuver until her calf ached.

"Glad to accept responsibility." McKenna cast a glance behind her. "The girls are ready when you are."

Selena leaned to kiss her mother. "You have brought me to this point, Mama. Without your strength, *nada. Comprendes?*"

"Oh, Selena." Fumbling with the beaded bag that matched her dress, Selena's mother wouldn't meet her glance. In her eyes, she'd done what any mother would do, but for Selena, her life's journey had been a miracle.

Harper poked her head in. "Hey, we're waiting for you to become Mrs. Selena Kirkpatrick. *Andale*, my future sister-in-law."

"Sister-in-law? I like the sound of that." Swishing her ruffles one last time, Selena nodded. "I'm ready."

Sofia arranged Selena's long white mantilla one last time, draping it perfectly over the comb their grandmother had worn for her wedding.

When they reached upstairs, the arches of the gothic church soared above them, saints and cherubs smiling down from the frescoes. For a second, Selena wished they had gone to Santa Fe to be married in the smaller Loretto Chapel. Then she caught sight of Seth standing at the end of the long aisle. Her future was in his smile. That's all she needed and her crazy stomach settled.

The organist struck up the traditional wedding march and little Lisa started down the aisle, flinging rose petals with each step. None of Seth's nephews wanted to be in the wedding party, but Lisa had been so pleased to be asked. She wore a child's version of the pale purple gowns worn by the women. Their lace bodices were dotted with dainty seed pearls and a peplum ruffle accented the long, trim skirt. One by one they paraded to the front and a murmur rippled through the church. They looked so beautiful and stylish.

Selena couldn't help but think back. Little girls can dream and she was no exception. Never had she ever imagined anything like this wedding. When she was a young girl, working in the fields, this was beyond her childish dreams. Gratitude filled her heart. A kiss on the cheek and McKenna stepped away, the final bridesmaid down the aisle. When she reached the altar, she turned left to join the others. McKenna's nod was Selena's cue.

"Oh, *Papá.*"

Her father patted Selena's hand while she clung to his arm. He looked handsome but uncomfortable in his tuxedo. *"Tenga una vida maravillosa, mi hija preciosa."*

Eyes damp, she nodded. Now she was the one unable to speak. Of course she would have a happy life. After all, she'd be sharing it with Seth.

Stepping out into the aisle, Seth beckoned her forward with his smile. Unbearably handsome in his tux, he was everything to her, the man who would love and cherish her forever. Best of all, he'd written his own vows. Oh, Seth might have trouble getting through them, but what did they care? She couldn't wait to hear them.

This past year they'd gone through so much to reach this point. Together they'd face the future, stronger as a couple than they ever could be alone. Smiling at the man who would soon be her husband, Selena took the first step.

THE END

Other Books by Barbara Lohr

Windy City Romance

Finding Southern Comfort
The Southern Comfort Christmas
Her Favorite Mistake
Her Favorite Honeymoon
Her Favorite Hot Doc
The Christmas Baby Bundle
Rescuing the Reluctant Groom

Man from Yesterday Series

Coming Home to You
Always on His Mind
In His Eyes
Still Not Over You

Past romances bloom again in the *Man from Yesterday* series, beginning with *Coming Home to You*. A family emergency calls Kate home. Can Cole Campbell give her reason to stay?

Coming Home to You

The thumping started when Kate Kennedy reached Greta's Gifts on Red Arrow Highway. Cheese curls churned in her stomach as she tapped the brakes. Almost home but something was wrong with the kayak strapped to her roof. Gravel crunching beneath the tires, she pulled into Greta's and parked. The sun bounced off the hood of her SUV, but a cool May breeze bathed her face when she cracked open the door.

Welcome to Michigan. Her eyes felt grainy from fourteen hours on the road, but she was home.

Stretching, Kate breathed in the lake, damp and beachy. The tightness in her shoulders eased. Pine trees caught a high spring gust and the familiar rustle made her smile. Her stomach gurgled. Not much to eat the whole ride from Boston except peanut butter and jelly, plus bags of cheese curls washed down with coffee.

Looking up, she exhaled. At least she hadn't lost Gator, her green kayak. A red security tie flapped in the breeze. Must have lost the other strap along the way. Kate scrubbed her face with hands shaking from all the caffeine. A semi roared past, kicking up dust. She tugged up the zipper on her hoodie.

"Doggone it, Gator."

The kayak slid a bit farther. Too bad she'd left her small kitchen stepladder in the Boston condo, along with a lot of other stuff.

When she yanked the remaining red band, it fell away in her hand. One frustrated shove and Gator retaliated, smacking her square in the chest before clattering to the ground. The pain bent Kate over like a paper clip. She almost didn't hear the door slam behind her.

Blinking furiously, she pulled herself up, grateful for the sunglasses. No way would anyone see Kate Kennedy cry. A man ambled toward her in work boots, worn jeans, and shoulders that tested the seams of a beat-up jean jacket. That walk looked familiar and her heart kicked up a beat. He wore aviator sunglasses, so no telling for sure. A black and white dog hung out of the pickup, Great Dane ears pricking forward. Big muzzle, big dog.

"Need some help?"

Yep, it was him. Kate's legs weakened. "No, I'm fine."

His eyes shifted to the kayak on the ground. "Doesn't look fine to me."

She fisted her hands on her hips. "I'm fine. And so is Gator." Her chest throbbed.

Blue eyes swept like a July wave over the tops of his sunglasses. "Gator?"

She swallowed. "My kayak. Seemed appropriate."

"I see."

But Cole Campbell had never understood why Kate wanted all her belongings named and in their proper place. Shoot. They'd been on the high school debate team together, and he didn't recognize her? Maybe it was her recent drugstore dye job. She'd had brown hair in high school. Now she ran a hand over blonde hair, crisp from two days of neglect.

He swayed back on his heels, a Good Samaritan with second thoughts. The two empty seats of the kayak stared up at them. "Lucky you didn't lose it on the road. Could have smashed into another driver. You need to batten it down."

"Thought I did. It was dark when I loaded it."

"Try doing it in the daytime. You could kill somebody."

"I left at midnight."

"Midnight?" He lowered the glasses and his eyes darkened.

Her chin came up. "Highway's quiet at night. Just the truckers."

"Exactly. Truckers. You think that's safe?"

None of his business. "I've, ah, probably got some rope in the back." She seriously doubted it.

"I'll be glad to help." Cole's attention shifted to her jeans. The corners of his lips lifted. "You saving that for something?"

Kate looked down. A cheese curl was caught in her crotch and she batted it away. No time for games. Especially not with him.

His eyes flitted from her to Gator and back. A stern mask slipped into place. Cole's teenage acne had left faint pockmarks that definitely didn't detract from his macho appeal.

Was he going to help her or not? Her chest throbbed. Could this day get any worse? The boy she'd lusted for in high school didn't even recognize her. Kate's throat closed. Nothing like feeling forgettable.

In two thrusts of his muscular arms, Cole had Gator back in the rack on top of her SUV. Disgusting how easy he made it look, but it gave her time to enjoy the view. Cole Campbell had definitely left "gawky" behind.

"Thank you."

Wheeling around, he caught her staring and grinned. "Got that rope?"

Her face burned. "Sure. I'll get it. Let me just check Bonita."

"Bonita?" He tilted his head.

"My car." One glimpse of the pretty blue SUV on the lot and she knew it was Bonita.

"Sure. Right."

Popping open the back gate, Kate launched herself into the tightly packed boxes and bulging trash bags. Her rear end felt big as a helium balloon.

"Finding anything? I might have something in the truck."

Feeling him hovering, she tried to squeeze her butt tighter.

When she heard the scratch of his boots, Kate thought maybe he was leaving. Her disappointment surprised her. After all, she wasn't at her best. If you're going to run into an old flame... well, a man you wanted to be your old flame... a girl should look hot, not sweaty.

Kate was sweaty. And not in a good way.

Finally, she climbed out empty-handed. Cole was ambling toward her with a roll of heavy gauge rope.

"That looks serious." Her mother wouldn't even be able to get a clothespin around this sturdy stuff, although she'd probably try.

"Want to stand on the other side and catch this?"

"Sure." *I'd hold anything for you. Like my breath.*

While Cole tossed a length of rope over the kayak, his dog watched from the pickup with mild interest. Grabbing the rope,

Kate threaded it back and he knotted it securely. "First, I like to tighten the bow and then the stern."

"You kayak?"

Whipping out a Swiss army knife, he cut the rope. "Way too much work. I sail."

Of course. She pictured an elegant yacht skimming Lake Michigan. Samantha McGraw would be rubbing her tan body against his. Kate didn't need the instant replay. Had enough of that in high school.

Cole worked with calm efficiency, the way he'd handled Student Council or Debate Club.

Oh, yeah. He'd handled their debate group just fine.

When he turned back, his eyes went to her hair. Smiling, Cole whisked something from the mess. Her breath left her body.

Maybe she was just tired.

Or maybe she was desperate for a man's touch.

He handed her a cheese curl. "You missed this."

"Great. Thanks." She jammed it in her jean pocket and then felt stupid. Was she going to press it in her high school scrapbook? Kate slammed her back gate shut.

Cole's eyes rested on the Massachusetts license plate. "Passing through or coming for the summer?"

"That depends." He still didn't know her? She edged toward the driver's door. "Thanks for your help."

Cole cocked his head to one side, like he was listening to her voice. "Sure. No problem."

"Got to get to an appointment." Maybe a shrink. She opened

the driver's door so fast she almost cracked herself in the mouth.

"Ah, huh. Well, good luck."

"Right. Thanks." Kate needed more than luck this trip. Without looking back, she peeled out and did a U-turn on Red Arrow. In bad need of a friendly face, she headed into town.

Driving toward Gull Harbor, Kate passed the ice cream parlors, restaurants, galleries, and gift shops that lured tourists. Some looked closed, and she hoped that was just seasonal. Winters could be hard on businesses, and this economy didn't help any.

Clancy's grocery store sat at the main intersection of Whittaker and Red Arrow, just next to Dressel's drugstore. Kate ducked into the grocery, grabbed a cart, and zipped through the aisles, snapping up basic necessities like OJ, milk, bread and cheese curls. Stopping at the deli counter, she picked up some sliced turkey and cole slaw. Should hold her for a while.

After stowing the bags in her trunk, Kate glanced across the street. The Full Cup sign swung above the frosted glass door. A cheese crown called to her from Sarah's shiny clean case. Hardly any traffic on Whittaker in early May and she sprinted across the two lanes. Kate pushed open the door of the bakery and breathed in the scent of warm, fresh pastries. No need to begin sensible eating now. Sour cream donuts, almond braids, cheese crowns and frosted brownies were neatly arranged behind the glass.

Freshly perked coffee perfumed the air with a hint of hazelnut. Definitely not the roadside stuff. Everything about the place looked the same, just the way Kate liked it. Her irritation eased. Would it be a cheese crown or a brownie? Kate was still deciding when Sarah whirled through the swinging door to the back, patting her brown curls. "Why, Katie Kennedy. Back so soon?"

"Couldn't stay away from your cheese crowns."

"I know. Me too." Laughing, Sarah wiped her hands on the apron around her ample waist. Miss Congeniality, hands down.

"Everything good? Boys and Jamie doing all right?"

Sarah had married Jamie Pickard, her high school sweetheart now serving overseas. They had two little boys.

"Yep, as far as I know. One cheese crown coming right up." Sarah handed over the largest pastry on the tray. She nodded toward the tables at the window. "Got time to chat? Coffee's free."

"Sounds like a plan." That run-in with Cole after all these years had left Kate's head fuzzy. She just wasn't ready to see her mom yet. After pouring a cup of hazelnut coffee, she slid onto one of the wire-backed chairs.

Sarah settled across the table with a sigh. "Your mother will be glad to see you."

"So you know about her stroke?" No secrets in this town. Today that felt good.

"How's she doing?"

"The therapists say she's improving."

"She'll be tickled to see you." Supportive to the bone, Sarah always had your back.

"Picked up groceries and thought I'd stop here." Kate's grin felt shaky. "Kinda tired. I started out late last night."

"A woman on the highway alone at night?"

"Cole Campbell already told me that was stupid."

"You're in touch with Cole?" Sarah's eyebrows lifted into her curly mop.

Kate brushed the crumbs from her jeans. "My kayak came loose, and he stopped to help."

"Really? Always so helpful. Cole's a mover and shaker here in town."

"Samantha must love that." Kate had heard Cole and Samantha married right out of college. By that time, Kate had been dating Brian for three years. High school friends pairing up had been old news.

But with Cole? Okay, the news gave her a twinge or two.

"They split up." Sarah stirred more cream into her coffee. "It's been tough for him the last few years. He has custody of their daughter."

Cole Campbell, a single father? "Thought the mom always gets the kids. Does Samantha live around here?"

"Nope. California, from what I hear. Anyway, Cole wants to move Gull Harbor ahead." Sarah glanced at the street outside. "Make some changes."

"Things look just fine the way they are." Kate took another bite of the sweet cheese.

"We've had a rough few years, Kate. Shops have closed or changed hands. Michiana Thyme was sold. Did your mom tell you?"

Kate shook her head, struggling to swallow. She always bit off more than she could chew. "Nope. She might be a little out of touch now." Craning her neck, Kate stared down Whittaker at the combination gift shop and diner on the main corner. Been there forever. Now it was sold? Her contentment at being home unraveled around the edges. "I was looking forward to their stuffed French toast."

"And I would have been right there with you, not that I need it. Loretta retired and moved to Florida to be near her son. No one wanted to take on the store."

"What's going to happen to the place?"

Sarah lifted a shoulder. "Town meeting pretty soon. Cole bought it. He's got plans. Your mom never said anything? She's always been so involved in Gull Harbor."

"She will be again. I have no doubt."

Sarah's eyes softened. "She'll be so glad to see both of you."

"Mercedes can't come. Too much going on with her company."

At least that had been the excuse. Kate didn't need to spell it out for her old friend. Eons ago, her older sister had borrowed an outfit from Sarah. The fluffy teal sweater and pants had been so pretty. After go-karting with friends, Mercedes returned it with oil stains. Never said a thing about it. Kate had been so embarrassed. Just another page from the book of Mercedes Kennedy. "I'm hoping Mercedes will be able to come soon."

"You Kennedy women are strong. Almost didn't recognize you, Kate. Like the blonde hair."

"What was I thinking? Crazy, right?"

"Maybe you need more crazy."

"Don't know if I'm ready for that." But change was bearing down on her, whether she liked it or not. This two-block street was all Kate had ever known in Gull Harbor. They'd hung out here at the Swirly Top, eaten Loretta's special orange ricotta stuffed French toast at Michiana Thyme and grabbed pizza at Touch of Italy. All the local kids got part-time jobs in the shops during the summer. "I want it to stay just the way it is."

"I don't know if that's possible, Kate."

Her coffee had turned lukewarm. The cozy hazelnut flavor was gone and a chill stole through the glass window. "Boy, it's cold. When will spring get here?" Kate pulled her hoodie tighter.

"We had a long winter." Sarah gave her a wry smile. "The ice floes didn't melt until just a couple weeks ago. Beach is going to be wide this year. Hope people can afford to rent cottages."

By Memorial Day, families would be bustling from store to store with bulging shopping bags. At least, that's the way it used to be. "How's your business?"

"Not bad. Course I have been taking more day-old pastries to the soup kitchens. Might as well have someone enjoy them, right? Gonna be here for a while? I'm sure the girls would love to see you. You probably have to get back, though. Husband, job, and all that."

Kate sucked in a slow breath, not quite ready to share the news. "So much depends on Mom's condition. I'm freelancing now, you know. Healthcare blogs."

"Right, you told me the newspaper had a layoff." A silence stretched until Sarah carefully swept crumbs off the table and into a napkin. "Well, then. You always liked to read, Kate. Come to our book group."

"Anybody I know?" Last thing she needed was a bunch of strangers asking questions.

"Chili and Carolyn Knight, who teaches at the high school."

"Chili? Don't think I would have passed Spanish without her." Chili would quiz Kate about verb conjugations until she could recite them in her dreams. "Carolyn? You mean Miss Knight? Still single and teaching at the high school?"

"Yep and then Phoebe and Diana. Both new to the area. You'll enjoy them. Phoebe has a hair salon and Diana opened Hippy Chick, a clothing store. Kind of cute."

Being with other women might be good for her. "Maybe. Thanks for mentioning it."

Sarah looked pleased with herself. "Good. We're meeting next Wednesday. My house at seven."

Whoa. "But I haven't read the book."

"'Bridges of Madison County.' I'll get it to you next week."

"Oh, I can wing that one." An old favorite, the novel was packed up in the garage of the condo, waiting for a destination address.

The door to the kitchen slammed open, and two little boys tumbled out, barefoot with t-shirts untucked. "Mom, Mom!" the first little guy called out, running to Sarah. "Nathan won't share!"

"Mine! These are my dinosaurs!" The other boy clutched some plastic figures to his heaving chest. The unruly hair marked them as Sarah's children.

"Double trouble." Sarah stared them both down. "Justin and Nathan, can't you say hello to Kate?"

The boys looked like they might consider it.

"Hello."

"Hi."

Sarah laid one hand on each boy's shoulder. "Where's Grandma Lila?"

Justin poked one finger back toward the kitchen. "Making something."

At that moment, a silver-haired woman appeared in the doorway, looking tired and more than a little frustrated.

"Sarah, I tried but they're bored." When Lila threw up both hands, white flour flew. "Hi, Kate. Good to see you."

"Boys, we're going to learn to share or your father will be very disappointed." Sarah wagged one finger before turning back to Kate. "Their daddy is a very brave soldier." The last was obviously said for their benefit.

"You must be so proud of him," Kate said. With his polished Italian loafers and weekly hair styling, Brian wouldn't have dreamed of going over to the Middle East. "Was Jamie in the reserves?"

Sarah nodded. "Called up, but he would have volunteered anyway. I've got a ton of chores ready when he gets back."

Kate checked the time. "I should get moving. Guess I'll take a cheese crown for my mom."

Shepherding the two boys toward their grandmother, Sarah bustled back behind the counter to retrieve Kate's cheese crown. "Mom, I think it's nap time."

Both boys howled.

Waving away Kate's money, Sarah squeezed her hand. "Oh,

don't be silly."

"I'll see you…"

"Next Wednesday," Sarah supplied. "My house. Seven o'clock."

"Right." Slotting something on her calendar felt good. Almost banished the embarrassment from running into Cole Campbell.

After all, wasn't he the one who should be embarrassed?

About the Author

Barbara Lohr writes contemporary romance with a flair for fun. Her *Windy City Romance* series is based in Oak Park, Illinois, delighting readers with spirited women who take on hunky heroes and life's issues. As they follow their hearts, these women take interesting jaunts to Savannah, Italy or Guatemala. Just around the bend of Lake Michigan sits Gull Harbor, Michigan, the setting for her *Man from Yesterday* series. Homespun love is the heart of this series, where women reconnect with the men they left behind. Both series are continually developed with stories that spring from readers' interest.

Family often figures in her stories. "No woman falls in love without some family influence, either positive or negative." Barbara lives in the South of the USA with her husband and a cat that claims he was Heathcliff in a former life. When she's not writing, she enjoys golf, kayaking, biking and cooking. Dark chocolate is her favorite food group, and she makes a mean popover. Sign up for her newsletter by going to her website. Friend her on Facebook or connect on Twitter!

www.BarbaraLohrAuthor.com

www.facebook.com/Barbaralohrauthor

www.twitter.com/BarbaraJLohr

A Word from the Author

Many thanks to the Romance Writers of America, whose members are generous with their knowledge base. The loops and forums of writers who address writing and publishing issues are invaluable to me.

To my readers, a heartfelt thank you. Your appreciation and support warm my heart. To my Street Team, you rock! Special thanks to Kay Crocker, Pam Mitchell, Debbie Sutherland and Jane Whitmeyer for their excellent proofing skills. To my growing First Readers Team, love you guys! Keep responding to my newsletters and be sure to enter my giveaways. I sure appreciate your interest and hope to continue to write books that take you on "journeys of the heart," as one of you mentioned.

Thanks to Kim Killion for covers that package my work perfectly. I look at those covers and think yes, my characters could walk right off that page. Your creative and technical skills are sure appreciated. And to Chris Hall, my editor. After untold hours of working n a manuscript, your suggestions and insight help polish my work.

For my daughters Kelly and Shannon, reading has always been a tie that binds. My grandchildren Bo and Gianna bring me such joy and of course pop up in my work. To my husband Ted, thank you for your love and support, especially when my computer has fits and you provide tech support. May we have many more wonderful years together with trips to Leopold's for ice cream.

CPSIA information can be obtained
at www.ICGtesting.com
Printed in the USA
FSHW022026010121
77331FS

9 780990 864264